Redefining Victory

Were things but only called by their right name,
Caesar himself would be ashamed of fame.

– Lord Byron

Redefining Victory

a post-truth novel

Anthony Stevens

Cover design: Maria Pesma

ISBN: 978-0-9955939-0-9

SILENOS BOOKS
Cambridge, England

https://silenosbooks.com

For Maria

PART ONE

The parting of the ways

It was a tragedy waiting to happen. John (youthful forty-two, professional, creative type) wanted to find out who he was. His wife, Mary, did not understand him. She assumed he must be going through a mid-life crisis, so she was trying her best to be a friend in need.

"A penny for your thoughts," she said, as they were driving along a winding country lane one damp and misty, grey November day.

"It's autumn," John responded gloomily. "The leaves are falling."

"Time marches on," said Mary, more in cheerful resignation than in explanation. Then the symbolism of his remark dawned on her. It offered a window of opportunity.

"John, you're still in the prime of life, you know," she added.

Nothing ventured, nothing gained, remained an article of faith for Mary. Falling into the depths of despair wasn't in anyone's best interests. But she immediately sensed the male body beside her stiffen in emotional rearguard action.

Her husband of fourteen years settled back into the shell of his stony silence, almost with a vengeance. Mary, he realised, would like nothing more than for him to open up his heart to her. Stubbornly, he refused to rise to the bait. Her own heart was in the right place, of course. But a relatively sheltered early life had conditioned her to a strong sense of family values (her parents had stayed together until she was all of twenty-one). She seemed not to realise that if he were to share his troubles with her, they would not be halved, but doubled.

A sense of sadness overwhelmed the thirty-nine year-old Mary. Had she been dreaming an impossible dream? At any rate, her wish list in life now seemed full of forlorn hopes. Over the past few weeks she had given John ample opportunity to air any grievances or make a clean breast of any dissatisfactions. But she had never known him less proactive where intimacy was concerned.

To make matters worse – as though fate just had to add insult to injury – they were on their way to the wedding of a close friend of hers. It seemed like only yesterday that she herself had walked down the aisle of a country church, knowing full well that a day would dawn when the honeymoon was over – not (as would have been all too obvious) in the literal sense, but in the words of.... But her train of thought had hit a mental buffer.

"John," she said, in a puzzled tone.

"What?"

"Is it 'For better *or* for worse'?"

"As in the plighting of troths?"

"Yes."

"What else?"

"'For better *and* for worse'?"

"Life has its ups and downs, true enough, not to mention its thick and its thin. But I think it's 'or'. After all, you wouldn't say 'For richer *and* poorer,' would you? It sounds contradictory – ignoring any longer-term swings and roundabouts, of course."

They were communicating! Suddenly, out of the blue, he was sounding like his old self!

"But it is 'In sickness *and* in health'! Isn't it? After all, not many people can say they've *never* been ill."

John turned to look directly at her. Her soul withered under his searing gaze. "Just what are you implying?" he snarled. "For the last time, I am *not* going to a shrink!"

"John! Keep your eyes on the road!"

But it was too late.

*　　　*　　　*

Two hours later, Mary stood outside talking into her Vodafone Smart Mini 8c with all the philosophical aplomb she could muster.

"Yes, I am looking on the bright side.... It certainly could have been worse, I know.... I am counting my lucky stars.... Yes, I know children are starving in Africa, it's terrible.... Ours, well, John's – *he* was driving, but I blame myself. Typical woman, don't say it.... For taking his mind off the job.... No, not like that, for heaven's sake, we *have* been married fourteen years! We were just talking. I managed to coax him out of his shell, got him to open up a bit, but he's so tired and emotional lately, and.... I don't know why.... Of course I've asked him.... He says he just wants some space and some time.... What do you mean, 'Married men are all the same'? You've only just tied the knot, how would you know? ... Of course, third time lucky, yes! Sorry, slipped my mind. Congratulations, by the way. I really am sorry we couldn't make it and I hope you'll be very – Oh, look, I've got to go, sorry, the ambulance has *finally* arrived, that's what we've been waiting here for.... Yes, like I said, we're both fine, not a scratch.... For the *other* driver.... I'm not sure. Alive anyway.... Yes, it is a shame. The AA man has been ready to give us a lift for a good hour now, but we couldn't not wait, could we? ... Oh, they've been and gone. Short staffed, they explained. Apparently you can make more in private security.... No, not a bit cold, we're inside a pub – well, right now I'm on the outside, to be completely honest, open and above board, but that's so you-know-who won't overhear – anyway, it's a Vintage Inn, you know, absolutely no horse brasses, lovely fire, another blessing to count. There's even a perfect view of the crash site through the window.... No, the police thought it best not to move him. John took a drink out. Anyway, got to dash, enjoy your honeymoon. Bye."

Mary felt uneasy. Her friend Louise had planted an unsettling question in her mind. Had she too got a typical married man for a husband? In words of one syllable (with one important exception), what did John *really* mean by "space" and "time"?

Mary was not by nature the jealous type. She was firmly convinced that a good relationship should be based on trust. Nonetheless she would have preferred it if John could have agreed to use his extra space and time in her presence, or at least in the house. That, in her opinion, would have been a reasonable quid pro quo for the concessions she was making. But he had flatly rejected her proposal.

On the other hand he was not actually going out any more often than he did before, which was two to three times per week, excluding working hours. He seemed to be satisfied with having more space and time *in principle*. At any time, however, principle could turn into practice, a fact which meant that Mary was living, on the plane of emotion, from day to day. And being the kind of person who liked to be able to plan for the future, she was not comfortable with feeling insecure.

She went back inside, having consumed quite enough fresh air for one day, then returned pensively to their table.

"Are these dead?" said a buxom girl, who was already gathering up their empties. The turn of phrase, so nonchalantly intoned, brought home to Mary the fact that she was after all lucky to be alive. It did not cross her mind that this might have been the onset of shock, hence her mood improved.

"Not a bad pub," John pronounced with masculine authority, primarily to the AA man with whom he was bonded by common sex, as they prepared to make a start on the long road home. "One of the oldest in the country, according to mine host. A thoroughly decent brew too. Interesting name, The Turning Worm, I don't think I've come across that one before."

"It's associated with a story, so they say," said the AA man. "It used to be called The King's Head, or maybe it was The Queen's Arms, I'm not rightly sure, but it's not material. About fifty years ago, the landlord of that era decided to change the name to the one you see before you now. Not long after, he murdered his wife."

"Oh, the poor woman!" Mary interjected, with a rush of empathy.

"How?" John inquired, remaining objective.

"Now that's the interesting part of the story, because no one ever found out how, dig as they might. Whatever he did, he made it look exactly like death by natural causes, so the main evidence against him was that sign."

The three of them looked up at the inn sign. It showed a large brown worm doubled back on itself, in a field of longish green grass, and a single distant bird in the sky overhead.

"The bird," continued the AA man, "is an allusion to the old saw, 'The early bird catches the worm'. He painted it himself, they say, not only to foreshadow the actual crime but also to make a kind of wry comment on the struggle for resources than underpins the survival of the fittest. It's a well-balanced composition to my eye, but I'm no expert. As for the wife, by the by, she was dead but wouldn't lie down, in a manner of speaking."

"You mean the pub is haunted?" asked John.

"So they say, but, speaking on a more personal level, I don't believe in paranormal phenomena. To my mind, the ghost motif in the tale is more symbolic than literal, although I'm no specialist on the subject."

"Symbolic of what?" John asked. Mary noted his interest with interest.

"Guilt. If you've read Émile Zola's *Thérèse Raquin*, you'll catch my drift."

They stood watching attentively as the other driver was lifted into the ambulance, on a stretcher. John and Mary wished him a full and speedy recovery, then climbed into the AA National Recovery truck, after pausing briefly to sadly survey the wreck of their one and only car on the back. As they drew away from the sleepy hamlet where they had just passed a small but not insignificant portion of their lives, the AA man picked up where he had left off.

"Yes," he said, "once married, always married, in a certain sense. There's many who'd like their freedom back, but it's not within the bounds of possibility, not one hundred percent, that is, not to my way of thinking, no. And it stands to reason, if you're not one hundred percent free, you're not free full stop, are you? I'm not speaking only of murder, I'm speaking of divorce too. My ex-wife's been haunting me for the past ten years. She can't let go emotionally, you see. It's a question of the psychological investment she made plus the fact that she's unable to negotiate the disbelief phase of the mourning process. She needs to get in touch with her true feelings so she can work through the pain and anger involved. But she keeps bothering me instead. Still, people are like that. How many of us really know what's best for us?"

"That's true," said John sadly, "all too true."

"All the same, life's a journey, isn't it?" said the AA man, as if he sensed the need to lift John's spirits. "We may not know where we're going, but we'll get there in the end just the same."

'33, Kitchener Grove, SW19,' Mary thought to herself. 'There's no place like it.'

A truth universally acknowledged is hard to come by in this day and age of multi-culturalism and, more to the point, student-centred learning. Relativism rules. Nevertheless, one that comes at least into most people's minds, when circumstances have gone beyond one's control and the quality of life seems to be fast ebbing away, is that *life goes on.*

Mary felt inclined to point this out to John, a few days after the accident. He seemed more down in the mouth than ever before. But the Volvo had been an old car, after all. They could afford a new one (on the never-never, that is). The odds were that he would lose his licence, but living in London he never drove to the office and she could take over the wheel for any excursions. As for the other driver, as fate would have it he was not too seriously injured; in all probability he would be up and around in a week or so. Last but not least, they had providentially taken out their insurance with one of the reputable companies, so there was nothing to worry about on that score.

"There's no use crying over spilt milk," she began decisively. "I know that PTSD is as real as it comes, to the sufferer at least, but in your ca..."

The way he looked up at her stopped her in her tracks. It was the tormented look of a lost soul.

"What is it, John?"

"I think you'd better sit down," he said.

She did so, keeping her eyes fixed interrogatively on his face. Then he stood up, turning his back forebodingly to her.

"I don't know where to begin," he began.

"Begin at the beginning."

"For Christ's sake, Mary, this isn't a story. This isn't some cheap novel. This is life! There is no beginning! There's no end either! It's all the middle! Life just goes on! We're forever in the middle and... well, it's as though I've forgotten how to swim, because I can't seem to keep my head above water."

Mary wondered if he was aware of the mixed metaphor. Probably not. The urge to unburden himself must have been overriding all other considerations. She decided against bringing it to his attention.

"Life is what you make of it," she pointed out instead. "In any case, swimming's much like riding a bicycle. You don't really ever forget."

But this fell on deaf ears.

"You've done nothing to deserve this," John went on, suddenly calm and collected. "You've been a tower of strength. But a shoulder to cry on is – sorry, but I have to put this most emphatically – *not* what I need."

He paused. Mary assumed, initially, that this was for dramatic effect. John was an accomplished, although unaccustomed, public speaker. Dutifully, she shifted her weight towards the edge of her seat. But the pause was lasting too long. He seemed to be stuck. She imagined him repeating '*not* what I need, *not* what I need,' inside his head.

"What *do* you need?" she prompted, sufficiently rather than most emphatically, not wishing to sound sarcastic.

"There's the rub," he said. "I've got no idea. Not in the sense of specific, well-defined, achievable goals."

"Not the slightest inkling?"

"Not even that. But...."

Clearly he was back in control of his pauses. Mary noted her cue.

"But what?" she responded.

"Whatever it is, it's not something you can give."

11

Mary's stomach sank while simultaneously a lump rose in her throat. She felt an emptiness in between. She prepared to fight back tears, but, strange to say, the need did not arise. For some weeks now she must have been unconsciously preparing herself for this moment.

John had started so he was going to finish. "Sometimes it's necessary to be cruel in order to be kind," he said, in a tone consistent with the demands of pent-up, conflicting feelings. "You know I'm not myself these days. I'm no good for you. You might find this hard to swallow, but I truly believe I'm not worthy of you. You deserve happiness. You've suffered enough. You're still young and attractive. You need someone who can give you quality time, a soul mate to be a true husband to you. A marriage made in heaven is just like a free lunch, there's no such thing, I know that. I know that sometimes it's necessary to work at a marriage. I've tried, God knows I've tried! I'm not claiming any moral high ground, that's all yours – along with the house, of course. I'll make my own way. I'm just not the man you married. Sometimes people grow apart. That's all there is to it."

He came over to her and took both her hands in his. "I'm sorry, Mary, truly sorry," he continued. "You've given me space and you've given me time, but the space and time I need is more than lies in the power of another half to give."

At last the hot, stinging tears welled up in Mary's eyes. In a fraction of a second she had slid her arms beneath his, pressed her palms against his manly shoulder blades and laid her head upon his masculine right shoulder, her face turned away from his neck thereby to establish a romantic rather than an erotic intimacy. In this manner she clung tightly to him.

"Do you still think of me as your other half?" she asked, hopefully.

12

"Old habits die hard," he said, placing both hands on her still well-moulded buttocks and firmly tilting his own pelvis closer to hers. "In fact, right now, I'd rather like to have my evil way with you... on the understanding that it won't change anything."

Mary broke away, seeking further details. Nothing made sense to her any more.

"You mean... make love?"

"Why not? I hope we're going to remain friends."

The maxim 'Life goes on' came back into Mary's mind. How much she had been through since she had wanted to cite it to John! Now it seemed more appropriate to cite to herself.

"One for the road, then," she said, kicking off her shoes and simultaneously unbuttoning her blouse. "I'm not wet though. I'll need a little foreplay."

*   *   *

"How was it for you?" John asked, some (even a good) ten minutes later, lying on his back, still naked (ignoring shirt and socks), on the sheepskin rug in front of the radiator. His chest was still heaving gently and he held a cigarette rakishly between his thumb and forefinger.

"Fine," Mary called from the kitchen. 'What's your poison?"

"The usual," John responded.

She brought him a whisky and soda, and a non-carbonated mineral water for herself.

"Just what the doctor ordered. We really could do with a bar in the living room," John observed.

Mary felt happy and warm inside. She had managed three reasonably bona-fide orgasms, good going under such emotionally draining circumstances, and John was talking about home improvements. Men are so simple, she noted inwardly.

13

"But I don't understand women," John said, his thoughts evolving convergently. "If you had just announced your imminent departure, pretty much as a fait accompli and permanent to boot, and on the assumption that I myself didn't want to get shot of you; then you went on to suggest one last roll in the hay, more or less for old time's sake, I'm not sure I'd be able to keep my end up if you know what I mean."

"Perhaps I know you better than you know yourself," Mary said with unabashed sweetness. The word "perhaps" was a little like having her fingers crossed behind her back, after all.

"The most total stranger probably knows me better than I know myself," said John, suddenly dejected. "Oh, Mary, I feel like someone who has lost his memory – except for the fact that I haven't. Do you understand?"

Mary had to confess that she did not. This, however, did not greatly trouble her. The John of old, the John she knew and loved, had always tended to become philosophical after satisfying his bottom-line need for carnal re-acquaintance. It was at such moments that the vast universe of unanswered, perhaps unanswerable, questions opened itself to him. She used to find his willingness to share the incomprehensibility of it all rather touching.

"I mean that my memories seem to belong to someone else. They're not really mine. There's a real me that hasn't got any memories – not yet. I suppose I must be having an identity crisis." He looked at her, then added: "There's no need to look so worried. It doesn't involve another woman."

Mary had indeed looked worried at the words "identity crisis". She had recently read about this syndrome in the *Sunday Times 'Style'* Magazine. Identity crises were relatively serious compared to the more common mid-life crises (with which they were sometimes confused), mainly because there were now so many available identities out there, mostly optional, but any pick'n'mix approach to self-definition was more than likely to fall between any number of stools. Medication was not called for but professional help could often restrain patients from rashly attempting to start what they all tended, symptomatically, to call a 'new life,' with all its attendant disruptions to their nearest and dearest. Unfortunately another of the classic symptoms, or indicators, was that sufferers strenuously denied being ill in any way. Moreover, the delusion that they were the only ones who could do anything to help themselves was virtually universal, although this rarely reached the degree of deciding to write their very own self-help book. She had every reason to look worried, she concluded. And what a fool she had been to suggest he go to see someone with qualifications and experience before she had realised the true gravity of the situation. This must have been a red rag to a bull, but not quite, thank goodness, the straw which broke the camel's back, since he was not only still here in the fold, but was also finally taking her into his confidence. (Mary basked for a moment in the trust which this implied.) On the other hand she was right to blame herself for the accident. They might have been killed and it would have been her fault! She, a mere lay person, had rushed in where angels fear to tread, just like a fool! She felt like kicking herself.

During this meditation John had in fact continued to take Mary into his confidence, without noticing that their tête à tête had become a one-sided affair. In the end, he turned towards her and placed his hand sufficiently high on her inner thigh for this to be understood as a gesture of satisfied appreciation rather than simply one of close acquaintance.

"So, although sex-life-wise no problem, that's not the be-all and end-all, and the long and the short of it

15

is that I now need to get a life – of the unhyphenated or all-encompassing variety," he summed up.

Mary apologised for having lost the thread.

"To cut a long story short," said John, just a touch ironically (for which Mary felt she could hardly blame him), "I was saying that the accident made me realise a thing or two. A fraction of a second in extremis certainly helps to clear the mind. One, we've only got one life, as a general rule. Two, from where I'm sitting, I'm in the driver's seat."

"And at the end of the day?" Mary said, resolutely encouraging him to be more explicit.

"It's more a case of the road," John obliged. "To call a spade a spade, I'm disengaging from the marriage."

"You don't mean...?"

"Yes, I'm afraid I do. One can't cherry pick one's nuptial delights, by definition."

"But what about the bar in the living room?" Mary asked. A fly on the wall would have assumed she was rushing headlong into denial. Not so. Instead, she was instinctively trying to focus on practical matters in order to maintain her emotional balance.

"Wishful thinking, more's the pity. Things like that not only add value, they help get a quick sale. And by the way, remember when I said that the moral high ground was all yours?"

"Yes," said Mary, acerbically. So the home improvements were not to be. How little she cared about her moral superiority now! What good was being put on a pedestal and left on the shelf?

"Well, I seem to recall throwing in the house as well. Heat of the moment, I'm afraid. I can't afford to have solvency problems. Liquidity, maybe – at a pinch and for a while. I really feel bad about it, but it's a case of press delete. OK?"

THREE

Oxford Street was filled with milling crowds, since there were only thirty-one shopping days to go to Christmas. Everyone seemed to have pre-set goals and unwavering priorities, to be confident, decisive and resolved. Everyone except Mary. She felt disorientated in this sea of teeming humanity and confused by the comfortlessly and joylessly flashing Christmas decorations. Everyone seemed complete, autonomous, satisfied with their lives and themselves and hence utterly oblivious to the close proximity of so many of their fellow mortals. Remarkably, this generated a perfectly unified collectivity of purpose, far greater than that attained in a political demonstration or by a crowd at a football match. This would have been transparent to an observer from outer space, but in a more down to earth and less proverbial perspective, the crowd might have been compared to a gas under pressure (popular science books being so popular these days), in the sense that while on the microcosmic level the behaviour of individual molecules is subject to quantum indeterminacy, statistical factors entail that Boyle's Law perfectly predicts the behaviour of the totality.

These however were not *Mary's* thoughts, for her head was spinning. Mary was, or seemed to herself to be, the only one who remained aware of the Other, in all its myriad shapes, sizes and ethnic origins. As a result, she was the only one who did not reach the higher level outlined above. The Other, that is, stood (paradoxically – since it was in such a rush) in the way of the Commodity, defetishising it completely. Hence her dizziness.

She regretted coming. Determinedly, however, she reminded herself of the reason she was there. Retail therapy, in the usual sense of the term, didn't enter the picture. After the bombshell of John's announcement that he intended to disengage from the marriage, as he had put it (as though, Mary reflected ruefully, their marriage had meant nothing more to him than an engagement), she had been grief-stricken, embittered, deeply depressed and unutterably angry, all – to make matters worse – at the same time. However, she was also determined to work through this phase. Her rational self told her that it would be better for all concerned if she approached the post-cohabitation stage of the separation process in a civilised manner. She would therefore buy John a Christmas present as usual.

But what?

She turned to the ten year-old girl standing beside her. "Haven't you got any idea what daddy might like?" she asked wearily.

"Chocolates," said the girl, whose name was Jennifer. "When's he coming home?"

It was a good idea. Chocolates did not imply close personal or family ties as, for example, an item of clothing would have done. They did imply continuing affection, however, but the brand-image ought not to be too closely associated with romantic assignations, such as Black Magic. Milk Tray had the right suggestion of down-to-earth, good old-fashioned common sense. She had no wish to imply that she was still clinging, nor even hopeful. No, the gesture was to seem one of acceptance. On second thoughts, Milk Tray could be construed as motherly, and that would be altogether too much of an abdication of her sexuality. She opted, in the end, for Thornton's Continental

Selection, which seemed to bespeak an educated, liberal outlook on life.

It was only when she had made the purchase and had just stepped out of the shop, in which they had had to queue for twenty minutes, that Mary realised her mistake. John had gone on a diet just two weeks before leaving home!

A penny dropped – but not on the pavement. 'So,' ran the gist of Mary's sudden insight, 'the *real self* John claims to be searching for is not synonymous with the *inner man*!' With this thought, she seemed to find herself inside a bubble. The madding crowd glided by – silent, slow, distant, unreal. She recalled Louise's words, "Married men are all the same". They now seemed words of wisdom.

"Are you going to answer my question or not?" said Jennifer, stamping her foot.

The ghostly crowd suddenly sprang to life – loud, quick, close, real.

"Well?" Jennifer iterated, folding her arms and standing feet spread apart.

"What question?"

"When is daddy coming home?"

Mary looked her daughter squarely in the face, resolving to be honest. But try as she might, she could not think of the words which might at least soften the blow.

"I'll put it another way, then," said Jennifer. "Does he still love you?"

Mary couldn't help herself. The pertinence of the unexpected question, together with the confirmation of what she had often heard on the radio, that children know more than one tends to give them credit for, and, last but not least, the impossibility of giving an answer in the affirmative, made her burst into tears.

Jennifer gave her mother a tissue. "Look at it this way," she said. "If he loves you, he'll come back. If he doesn't, you'll be better off without him. The important thing is that he still loves *me*. I'm a child so my interests come first."

The childish logic was unassailable. Mary felt deeply ashamed of her egocentric attitude to the breakdown of her marriage. Jennifer had made her realise that the world is full of other people, to the extent that the thronging crowds no longer oppressed her. On the way to the bus stop she even stopped to buy a copy of *The Big Issue*.

*   *   *

When she grew up, Jennifer was going to be either a veterinary surgeon or an air stewardess, she had not yet made up her mind, but she was certain that she was never going to get married. She preferred animals to boys, except for some invertebrates which were equal. School was OK, though, and at least now no one could tease her because she only had one home. At school she read books about a child her age with only one parent who was in a wheelchair (the parent, not the child) yet who was normal in every way (the child, not the parent) although her reading age was twelve and a half (Jennifer's, not the girl in the book's). She was nearly old enough to read novels, her teacher, Ms Pringle, said, but Jennifer was suspicious. She knew that novels were bigger than storybooks not only because they used bigger words, but also because they were about bigger people with bigger complications in their lives, and although there were special, quite short novels for readers who weren't really grown-ups yet, you still had to be not just a child any longer to be able to understand all the emotions, but Jennifer didn't feel ready to be a teenager in spite of her reading age, since she hadn't started her periods like Tracy, whose reading age was only eight, had. But Ms Pringle was like that, very serious about everything and with no concept of play. For example, she had explained to the class how she had had to plan carefully and responsibly to get pregnant, due to her orientation, which she couldn't explain, but Jennifer thought it must be the opposite of westernisation which Ms Pringle said was very bad.

Jennifer found it interesting how one thought always seemed to lead to another so that often you couldn't remember what you were thinking of even a few moments ago because it was so different to what you were thinking of now. This was what made writing more difficult than reading. She didn't have a writing age though. If you tried to write down your thoughts as they came into your head, you couldn't, because your hand wasn't as fast as your brain, so you also had to think about *which* thoughts to write down. On the other hand you never forgot what you had just written because you could always read it again. Then there was another problem. Some of her thoughts, like the thoughts she was having now, were in words, but others weren't, they were in pictures instead. Or, to make things *even more* complicated, if she thought for example of her grandmother she thought of tasty cooking. Though not only that, of course. When she came out of school and sometimes at weekends too she stopped at her grandmother's where she felt much more sure of being noticed. She was really, really lucky that her grandmother lived nearby, just three streets away, something which would have been impossible in a school storybook, not just the ones about all the different ways of being normal but even if her grandmother had been a witch, because negative stereotypes weren't allowed even more (or should that be less?) than positive ones were (or should that be weren't?). In fact now she could say she was going to have three homes, not just two, provided that her father did still love her, so she would have to be careful not to show anyone any favouritism.

By this time, the bus was approaching their stop. Jennifer stood up and pushed the bell. She was quite sure her mother would have failed to do so; her mother was so obviously *completely* lost in thought that she probably didn't even realise yet that they had actually got on the bus.

FOUR

Meanwhile, one week into his new life, John was beginning to discover for himself the truth of the AA man's philosophy of the ties that bind. It was not that he missed the domestic convenience of having company on tap. It was not that he missed the conjugal right to the eponymous rites. Nor, to do her full credit, could he say that Mary was clinging, nor overplaying the role of victim, nor broodingly vengeful, nor even was she attempting to control him by means of the fruit of their loins. On the contrary, she was being thoroughly decent about it. But a marriage is more than most people imagine, at least until they try to leave one behind them. A marriage is not merely built on common values and pursuits, mutual respect and support, shared time and tasks, freedom of information as to whereabouts during absences from hearth and home, feedback sought and proffered as to what to wear to external functions, unconcern concerning what is worn otherwise, and, last but not least, realism with respect to the possibilities privately suggested – now and then – by fantasy. A marriage is also an efficient means, from the vantage point of the individual as distinct from the partnership, of maximising the kind of benefits that bear precise relation to costs.

Working through the pros and cons like this, John realised that if he had been over the moon about Angela, or even simply obsessed by her, he would not have been reviewing his newly reduced circumstances in such a clear-sighted way. This reflection confirmed him in his faith that he had been perfectly honest with

Mary. His identity crisis did *not* involve another woman. He had not felt inclined to mention the existence of Angela to his wife for the simple reason that Mary would have got hold of the wrong end of the stick.

Angela, in whose bed he was now passively lying and in whose arms he had just actively lain, was a twenty-four year-old graduate student of literature with red hair, green eyes and a dynamic personality. She had walked into John's life, by way of his office, some six months before.

John was an image-consultant. Although most of his clients were corporate, of late an increasing number of individuals from various walks of life had been waking up to the benefits of the service he provided. But Angela was the first from the ivory towers. She was ambitious and impatient to secure a lectureship at a top university as the first step towards being translated into many different languages. Her curriculum vitae was outstanding, she had expounded, but for some reason she was falling at the last hurdle, the interview, of which she had had two so far.

"Have you tried to diagnose the essential problem yourself?" John had asked.

"I've done better than that. I've deconstructed it," Angela replied. "How quaintly post-pre-Socratic of you, presupposing there's such a *thing* as an *essential* problem. Don't get me wrong. It's like being curled up cosily in bed with Aristotle. Don't tell me, I bet you still think you think therefore you are, don't you?"

John had heard the maxim before and felt unable to fault it.

"Ha, ha, ha!" laughed Angela. "You *are* where you do *not think*," she corrected him. "It's elementary Lacan."

John did not entirely understand what she was getting at.

24

"Thank God for that!" Angela expostulated. "The signified's a bugger of an opportunist, rears its ugly phallic head and tries to sneak in by the back door just when the *glissement* of the signifier is *really* flowing freely."

John went on to wonder what the relevance of all this was to the subject in hand, then, for some reason, he felt the need to explicate: "I mean to your... problem".

"The subject in hand! You're lucky I'm not a *practicing* psychoanalyst, using language as carelessly as that! Let it get out of hand! *If* we don't explode the hypostasised unity asserted monosemically through the mythicised etymologylessness of the archaic sense in which you imagined *you* used the word but in which *the word used you*, we'll get nowhere very fast. And what the hell do you mean, '*my* problem'? Of course, I *know* what you *meant* to *mean*. I'm not usually in the habit of resorting to clichés, not outside inverted commas, *but*, in a case like this, *one* option would be to remind you that the Irish long had an English problem."

Angela's forthright speech was beginning to make John feel role-reversed, but without his consent. "In that case, I'm really not sure that I can help you," he announced with as much assurance as he could muster, pushing the previously completed personal details to one side and (determined as he was to retain at least the outward form of a gentleman) preparing to stand up.

"But that's exactly *why* you *might* be able to," Angela went on. "Authority pisses me off. If your discourse *was* dominant, I'd put the boot into the gap between your enunciation and your enounced. I can't resist it. It's my default nature to kick against the pricks. Can't you *see*?"

For a moment, time stood still while, sitting on the other side of his Danish-design real wood-finish desk with its perpetuum mobile significantly at rest, John saw a helpless little girl.

They had not started a relationship immediately, however. When, during that first meeting, she had so unexpectedly broken through her fixation with discourse-analysis to utter that cri de coeur, that *appeal to be seen*, John had felt deeply moved and it had crossed his mind that Angela desperately needed the approving gaze of a father figure in her life. If so, then by definition she was not yet mature enough to admit this to herself. To have done so at this stage of her personal and professional development would have caused the collapse of her defence mechanisms and hence a painful theoretical reorientation. It was too early, therefore, to make any move. So he closed the conference by telling her that it would almost certainly require several more meetings at frequent intervals if he was to be able to work out an effective strategy, the case being a difficult – but also, from his side, a most attractive – one.

When she had gone, he went through her personal details, reading that she was preparing a doctoral dissertation on 'sub-textual polymorphic perversity in the textual actualisations of the Mills and Boon metatext' with particular interest, for, thanks to Mary, whose understanding of domestic duty included giving an occasional boost to her husband's ego, John knew full well that the early forties was a most attractive age, in men, in the hot and humid world of fiction by women, for women.

*   *   *

Now, six months on in time, here he was in bed with her nestled beside him, without needing to feel a jot out of order, let alone a tittle conscience-stricken. He was a free man. And she was a liberated woman. It certainly sounded a good match. Why then had he sensed a cooling of her ardour, a certain reserve in her abandon and, last but not least, a reduction in the number of her throes? And why the bed, of all places? "Variety is the spice of life," she had said, either in explanation or irony. How could she possibly experience her usual 'jouissance unconfined' in a single bed? And now, in what she called without a trace of jocularity the 'post-play' phase of their intimacy, she was reading a book. That in itself was not unusual, but on this occasion she was not immersed in anything which could remotely pass by the name of écriture. She was reading a *novel*! She had explained to him often enough that she never read novels, since the point was to *re-read* them, and that this was something best done by way of readings already published. But the fact which John found most difficult to comprehend, after all he had learned in their previous bouts of post-play, was her selection of novel with which to lapse.

"Not that I've read it since I was thirteen, and then not in its entirety," he probed her gently, "and far be it from me to have an opinion of my own on such a subject, but I would hardly have thought that *Lady Chatterley's Lover* was your cup of tea."

"Really?" Angela replied laconically, although more loudly than one who is, in the truest sense of the word, absorbed.

"Isn't Lawrence on the unreconstructed side of the fence?" he pressed his point home, yet the more tentatively, to the extent that the thrust of his question might not even have been construed as rhetorical.

"I don't understand how a *fence* can be *un*reconstructed on *one* side only," Angela quipped, to make him feel, once again, that he was more a brontosaurus than a mere bull in the china shop of the signifying chain. "But I've an interview Friday. Oxford.

I've been doing *your* job for you, and not only *in* bed. As to your province, the image-thing, talking about Lawrence at a mindopsy would be *pretty* Islamic-fundamentalist prospects-wise, that's kamikaze in your-generation-speak, *but* I think I can pull it off. Cunning plan, really – that's wheeze to you. *They're* looking for something standing-out, rather than *outstanding, that's* been my mistake. Do you see?"

"Up to a point," John replied in what he considered to be measured tones. "I'm reasonably clear about the day and place of the interview." And at least he understood now why her mind had not been fully on the job a little earlier in the evening. It had been on her career.

"A sarcast is the lowest form of twit," she retorted, tweaking his nose playfully, though Angela's sense of play was a little robust for a rugby fan such as John. The withdrawal of his nose, however, seemed to get through to her. "Look, you've been good both to and for me," she reassured him. "Without you, I would never have realised that the clitoris isn't the alpha and the omega, so it would never have occurred to me to re-read Lawrence, who nobody *dares* mention any more, let alone dip *into*, so I would never have realised that, in order to get a job, I needed to shock *them* with *what* I say rather than *the way* that I say it. Sacrilege, I know, but is it so wrong to sell *out* in order to *sell* your*self*?"

John warmed to the confessional turn taken by their conversation. "You know, after making love..." he began.

"'Fucking,' don't you mean?" Angela waved the shamelessness of the minor aristocracy vaguely in his direction.

"You can't teach an old dog new tricks," John pointed out with middle-aged candour. "A youth misspent combining fucking with hell, you see."

"I referred to the word. In its post-1960 and pre-1066 sense."

"So did I, I believe. Anyway, following our... sexual intercourse, I was lying here think..."

"There's no *verb* form of sexual intercourse, is there?" she interrupted, but, as interruptions go, it seemed to be unconscious of being such. "It's not the 'inter' part – think of interacting – nor the 'course' part – think of the blood coursing through your veins – still, interact is not a noun *too* – but interview is! Yes!!! *And* you can interview *someone*, or *be* interviewed! Jesus, I think I'm on to something big! It's a bloody great gaping hole in the Symbolic Order! The question is *why* does lexi-patriarchy need to repress the intercoursing of, and by, each other? I'll tell you why! *Because* of the phonemic associations, *inter, into, in, internal* – which would make a *man* feel reciprocally penetrated, obviously! *Now* all I've got to do is, come Friday – I don't mean *I've* got to *come* Friday/perhaps I do – anyway, *is* work round to *this*, and *Lawrence* is the way, because it *explains* the defence mechanistic pathology of his nouveau-proletarian four-letterism! Fucking hell, I think I've got the job!"

"Doesn't that depend, at least partly, on the opposition?" John asked naively.

Angela appeared not to hear this, as though to measure out in full the mile by which he had missed the point that, in her case, the only opposition was her own tragic flaw, underperformance under interview. But being ignored reminded John that he had previously been trying to tell her something. Should he try again? If at first... he told himself.

"*Anyway,*" he stressed proactively, "after expletive deleted, I was lying here musing upon this and that, as one does, when my mind found itself up against the state of the economy. Apparently the recession is now official. We're not just talking downturn any more. You know and I know that image is the last thing one should economise on in hard times, but the way of the world is not always as rational as a thinking being might think. In short, business is bad. As yet there's no light at the end of the tunnel. I'm a realist. I know I have to cut my coat according to my cloth. I'm not averse to counting the pennies. But now I'm shelling out on rent as well as the mortgage, not to mention maintenance, so should I ask Mary to move into something more compact?"

"Why not?"

"Sorry?"

"I said 'Why not?'"

"Ah. I see. Yes." To all appearances, he had her attention. "Well, there's just one snag," he said, capitalising on the fact. "Or rub if you prefer."

"What's that?"

"Would it be fair on the child?"

"What child?"

"I have a daughter."

"You have a daughter?"

"Yes. A little girl."

"Why didn't you tell me?"

"I didn't think of it. Was it relevant?"

"You didn't think it was relevant that you have a daughter?"

"I told you about my wife."

"What's that got to do with it?"

"It's my wife who doesn't understand me, not my daughter."

"Get out of my place!"

"Why?"

"You're a complete and utter bastard!"

"Why?"

Angela got decisively out of bed, gathered his clothes derisively from the armchair where they lay, and threw them divisively at him.

"Why? Why? Don't you realise I need a father figure I can *respect*? Don't you realise I need the kind of older man whose parenting skills I can *believe in*? Don't you realise that if I stayed with you now I'd have to face the fact that you're just like my *real father*? Don't you realise that that might even be what I *really want*? Don't you realise that if I let myself get that involved I'd only start waiting for you to *desert me too*? Don't you realise that the resulting panic attacks would cause me to *fail in my career*?"

She picked up one of his shoes, which, in her hand, became a signifier of the fact that she was not waiting for an answer. He managed to dodge it, slid expertly from the bed like a snake shedding its skin in a forest fire, re-lived Adam's first shame as briefly as possible by thrusting various limbs through various openings with remarkable if not always perfect accuracy, and found himself sufficiently decently dressed by the door in a time which would have been more than respectable had such an event formed part of the Special Olympics.

Angela had her nose pointedly in D. H. Lawrence.

Was this the parting of the ways? Was this the end of a chapter in his life? Had they just been ships which pass in the night? Questions such as these came thick and fast to his mind. Would they continue to do so? Could he live with such uncertainty? Would he have to wait for time to tell?

No, he resolved. But rather than ask her now, he would call to find out – after her interview, when Angela ought to be less stressed.

FIVE

33, Kitchener Grove, SW19, was a fully modernised three bedroom semi-detached house in a mature residential area, close to a wide range of amenities. The property offered full family sized accommodation, with shower room and WC separate from the main bathroom to help reduce the morning queue. The spacious open plan reception and dining area, with fitted carpet and traditional bay window, was ideal for entertaining or simply sharing precious moments, while year round personal space was guaranteed by the centrally heated and double glazed conservatory, which opened on the prospect of the delightful ninety-foot rear garden with bird table. The extended designer kitchen and breakfast room offered the full range of appliances including integrated coffee grinder, water filter and colour coded recycling bins. Benefits included garage and state of the art intruder detection system.

Mary sat in the master bedroom, which now, alas, also guaranteed her personal space, courageously looking through old photographs on her laptop. One day in the future, she told herself maturely, her present painful memories of happy times with John would become happy memories once again, or at least be recollections in tranquillity. Her purpose, however, was not to rehearse for such a day, which, after all, would first require the building of a new life. That was something easier said than done: new lives don't just build themselves, as she was well aware, but she had not yet even thought of where to begin. Instead, her purpose was altruistic – to select and print out some mementos of times past for John, for old times' sake. Lest he forget. She had been stoutly working her way back down the years, encountering ever younger selves in what seemed ever happier times, and was just bracing herself to open the folder which documented the happiest day of what, sadly, was no longer her current life, yet was not, tragically, a previous one (or not yet), when the doorbell rang.

What Mary first perceived on opening the front door was a familiar yellow truck parked in the road outside, for the vibrant primary colour stood out in the misty, grey day. This immediately helped her place the familiar, weather beaten face of the man who stood on her threshold and went some way to explaining the familiarity of the expression on it, but it did not entirely account for the bunch of yellow roses held out towards her.

"Hello, I was just in your area, passing through," said the AA man.

"Is this a follow up service?" Mary asked.

"In a manner of speaking, yes," he replied.

"I'm afraid my husband's... away. At the office."

"Oh, what a shame. Still, my fault, calling at two p.m. on a Wednesday afternoon." He paused, then proceeded by way of justification, "But I was in your part of the world, so to speak. My work... my life on the road, as I prefer to call it – I'm a rolling stone by nature as well as trade, you see... it takes me to places like that – by chance, as you might say, though sometimes I think it's destiny."

On the word "destiny," Mary reached out unconsciously and took the yellow roses – without even saying thank you. "What is?" she asked, her voice tightening in a note of heightened tension.

"Everything. Everything that happens to us," the AA man expanded, now that his hands were free. "Everything that happens, happens, and everything that doesn't, doesn't. It stands to reason, either we say what didn't happen could've and what did might not've, or we say what did had to and what didn't couldn't. Now, to my way of thinking – not that I'm any kind of authority – chance, or randomness, is just what we can't explain. It doesn't have independent existence or intrinsic being, not in itself, which leaves only the one option."

"But what about free will?"

"Well, suppose, hypothetically, you were to invite me in for a cup of tea."

"Oh, I am sorry," Mary apologised.

"No, no, no," the AA man insisted. "When I say 'hypothetically,' I mean 'hypothetically'. Of course, that's not to say I don't have an interest in the actual. In fact I'd love one, yes, thank you. Shall we go inside, then? Anyway, you inviting me in like this, for a proverbial cuppa, nothing more, nothing less, could nevertheless be a fork in the road, to use a turn of phrase, in the sense that the whole of the rest of your life might now be different than if you'd not done so, but nonetheless – and this is the crux as far as the problem of free will is concerned – it might turn out to be the only possible solution of the puzzle of your life up to now. Nice living room. Very tastefully furnished. Cum dining room, I see."

"Thank you," said Mary, warming to the masculine way in which, without waiting to be asked, he had sat down in the most comfortable armchair, leaning casually back, legs frankly spread, arms extended proprietarily over her best upholstery, even the fingers of the hands spread out uninhibitedly to occupy maximum space. Her heightened tension was lowering appreciably. Men seemed to her so materially grounded, so at one with their mass, so at ease with gravity. The fact that she had missed this of late awoke in her a desire to give, or at least to display the fact that she had much to give: "Which would you prefer," she asked, heading kitchen-ward. "Earl Grey, Yunnan, Lapsang Suchong, Green Gunpowder, or, for retro, Brooke Bond PG Tips; I've a variety of healthful herbals too."

"What kind of cups will you serve it in?"

"I was rather thinking of mugs," she called from within her domain.

"Ah, then I'll have an instant coffee, white, one sugar, if it's all right with you. You've never been to Japan, then?"

"No."

"Nor have I, to put it bluntly, but I've read all there is to read about the Tea Ceremony. *Teach Yourself The Tea Ceremony*, *The Tea Ceremony For Beginners*, *Bluff Your Way In The Tea Ceremony*, you name it, I've read it, although that doesn't make me a Master, since the Tea Ceremony, they say, isn't something you can learn out of a book, not one hundred percent, that is, no more than you can, for example, bull fighting or hang gliding. It's not like chess, to put it mildly. There are rules, of course, but it doesn't reduce to the rules. As I understand it, the secret is humility. You mustn't think you're serving your guest, you see. You're serving the tea. Nice kitchen. Very tastefully appointed. Breakfast room too, if I'm not mistaken."

"You're serving the tea to your guest, I suppose," said Mary, to establish the global view. Not only did she not mind that he had followed her to the kitchen, she was glad. He stood in the doorway, his left arm bent over his head, thus to lean against the doorframe in what might have been the relaxation of Atlas. He had a way of making himself at home, that is, that made her feel at home with him.

"No, no, I mean it's like you're the *servant of* the tea, not the servant of your guest. Everything you do is for the tea. But the trick, as against the secret – that's a basic distinction in Japan, by the by – is that you don't do anything for the tea at all. Don't get me wrong, but you don't light the fire in order to make the tea. Instead you light the fire in order to light the fire, if you know what I mean."

"I know exactly what you mean," said Mary. "I often put the kettle on but then I'm not completely sure I did put the kettle on till I hear it, you know, making a noise."

"That's modern life for you," said the AA man, removing his arm from the doorframe and taking a single, telling step actually into the kitchen.

"Exactly," Mary went on, responding to the ease with which their conversation was flowing. "We're all too busy, aren't we? We've all got too much on our minds, trivial things mostly, things to do, chores, duties, ambitions, dreams, so we live for the future, never realising that tomorrow never comes. So we fail to live *in* the present, we fail to *live the moment*. Yes, that's modern life in a nutshell."

The AA man had by now taken several more steps towards her. Mary was no expert on proxemics, but she understood the difference between a man making himself at home with an armchair or a doorframe and one with the same sense of entitlement towards her.

"Or perhaps by 'modern life' you rather had in mind the wide range of domestic appliances?" she said, by way of damage limitation and on the assumption that what had inflamed him was her immediately preceding speech. In retrospect, that projection of a laid-back, aging-hippie-housewife seemed entirely out of character, explicable only as momentary possession by the spirit of John Lennon.

But she could think of no explanation for the unpremeditated and radiant smile she felt herself flashing in his direction. She was not inclined to think the unthinkable.

The AA man's Mr Hyde was the strong, silent type and offered no verbal clarification. He took her in his arms instead. Her first thought was resistance (or at least a moment or two's reluctance), but she wavered too long a moment in selecting the precise tone with which to say 'No' – not surprisingly, since it needed to be unequivocally assertive but at the same time free from sweeping feminist generalisations – allowing, thus, the sharp, sour tang of oil to penetrate her nostrils, wherewith her knees informed her she was lost.

"No," she whispered, in an unpremeditated tone of a fast ebbing ability to premeditate a thing, "not here."

Too late, he was already lifting her on to the ample and gleaming work-surfaces. She was aware only of his hands, in which she felt herself rapidly becoming analogous to putty. They were not like John's. They were not the remote instruments of a centralised brain. His hands knew for themselves where to go, what to do, instinctively. Each had a will of its own, yet they cooperated like hunting wolves. One pushed the toasted sandwich maker to one side as the other sought out the fastener of her bra. The former was then called urgently to reinforce the latter, which, a moment or two later, broke away accurately to locate her right thigh, where it quickly determined that she was wearing pantyhose rather than stockings as such. Instantly possessed of this same knowledge, his right hand left her now uninhibited breast and intuited the position of the zip fastener of her skirt, with which it engaged in a brief skirmish. Triumphant, it joined its mate in firmly grasping the upper reaches of the tightly fitting item which up till now had forbidden his trespass. Perfectly synchronised, they then jiggled the immediate object of his desire to light, although elaborately laced ankle-high boots prevented

Mary's reduction, even from the waist down, to the full Edenic dress-code.

One of the AA man's hands had just turned to the remaining hurdle of his own trousers, the other preferring to keep in touch with Mary, when, in sudden agitation, her phone effused the kind of tune that cannot equally be called a melody.

"Ignore it," he said, on the verge of achieving, with the help both of gravity and of something which resembled marching on the spot, his own partial but sufficient undress. By quirk of fate, however, she had left her phone on the very kitchen counter upon which she was now recumbent, not even at an arm's length away. This made it entirely feasible just to glance (out of pure curiosity) at who was calling while remaining a full ninety-nine percent able to 'live the moment,' as she had previously and, she was now beginning to feel, felicitously defined it. But that was a miscalculation, for the caller was Louise. Having missed her wedding, Mary instinctively felt that it would have sent entirely the wrong signal to miss her first call since as well.

"Hello, Louise, welcome back…. And *I've* got things to tell you, but look, I'm in a bit of a strange position right now – situation, I mean, rather a sticky one, potentially, something on the point of boiling over. I'll call you back in five – no, sorry, make that forty-five minutes! OK?"

SIX

Louise had had a truly wonderful time. She would recommend Africa, on the strength of Kenya, without reservation (in the sense of unreservedly, since their luxury boutique safari lodge had been full). All's well that ends well. Or better, all's well that does nothing worse than get off to a bad start; for while sitting, seatbelts fastened, on the plane, waiting for takeoff, Louise had experienced a pang of... no, more a twinge of... no, more a disconcerting sense of... contradiction, yes, that was the word. Howard, panic free as ever, was immersed in a book (called *Kenya*) and chose that very moment, when there was no turning back, to share the fact with her that the very best time to see the country's main attraction, nature red in tooth and claw, was the very early morning! Dawn, no less! But they were on honeymoon! True, it was her third, but deep down Louise remained a conventional soul. But Lady Luck had smiled on them, fortunately, for, on arrival, the receptionist announced that due to recent intense safari activity, the big cats were now opting for high noon to do anything more suitable for dynamic action shots than laze around. They found the heat of the midday sun the lesser evil. The safari companies were revising their schedules accordingly, of course. Well, to cut a short story even shorter, within a mere three days they had not only seen but bagged, digitally, all the Big Five, plus a few Maasai as a bonus, all without needing to vacate the nuptial bed indecently early! And by the way, it was true what they say about the African sky, it was much, much wider than any Louise had come across in the Home Counties. To sum up, she was sure that Mary must have seen *Out of Africa*, and she could now vouch for the fact that it really had been shot on location, that being the only conceivable explanation of her multiple, almost rolling, sensations of déjà-vu and the way Robert Redford kept coming into her mind while crossing the Maasai Mara by minibus.

Thus, in something of the way that a drowning man's life is said to pass before his eyes, or at least with something of the necessary speed, the burden of Louise's unconsummated phone call was reviewed in her mind's ear. Her phone's essential place in her life became again the coffee table beside her. Not that Louise was drowning, but she had lost *some* bearings. Forty-five minutes was unheard of! She had known Mary since school. Mary was the kind of person to unhesitatingly turn the cooker off when she, Louise, called after nothing more than a day trip to Whipsnade Zoo.

"Howard," Louise said, from deep in her thoughts.

"Louise," Howard responded with elaborate personal address – they were still in the process of bonding as a domestic unit.

"Yes?" Louise came back to him, though not, apparently, entirely to herself. She seemed to have forgotten her own role as prime mover.

"Your throw, I think," said Howard, his patience still firmly rooted in affection. "Something up?"

"It's Mary. She's in some kind of... trouble."

Howard was the chivalrous type, being noticeably taller than the norm. "Anything I can do?" he inquired.

"But I don't know what kind of trouble."

"Ah. That complicates the picture, although it fails to thicken the plot," Howard observed critically. "Any intuition to pass on, you being a woman. Mary likewise, that should help. As a man, I can only deduce. Nothing much to go on yet, though."

40

Louise paced up and down twice, four steps in each direction, presumably as some kind of ritual aid to better comprehension. Then she turned to Howard, looked him squarely in the face, and said: "She sounded distracted, unable to concentrate. That's a common symptom of depression."

Howard preferred to leave no stone unturned. "Mother's ruin?" he suggested.

"No, her articulation was accurate. But her voice was... breathy.... Of course! Shallow breathing. Due to anxiety, in all probability. Yes, there *was* a note of desperation. Even... feeling lost, out of control." Louise took four more steps in one direction, quickly followed by four in the reverse direction (first having turned around). She then confronted Howard, both posturally and facially as before. "John's at what they used to call a dangerous age, isn't he?"

"Following the way of all testosterone, you mean. Poor Mary. Poor if you've hit the nail on the head, that is. She has fear of freedom written all over her."

Oh my God!" Louise cried out suddenly.

"It's worse than you thought?" deduced Howard.

"Yes! It's nearly Christmas! Poor Mary! We've got to do something!"

Louise's allusion to the forthcoming seasonal peak in the suicide rate was lost on Howard. Still, he tried to respect what he took to be a rush of goodwill to all men. "Well, we are a *team* now," he said, affirmatively. "Let's put our heads together, as a change from our genitals."

*   *   *

Louise had met Howard at a conference on 'Escalation Management in the Divorce Process' just over a year before. As a lawyer with a special interest in situations of marital breakdown, Howard had interpreted the phrase 'Escalation Management' not so much in terms of controlling or limiting escalation as in terms of making the most of it. Louise, on the other hand, as a social and life skills therapist, firmly believed that escalation could and should be avoided by means of non-adversarial forms of words. One evening in the bar, Louise had commented that she had found that afternoon's presentation on 'Sincere Intonation in the use of Empathy Statements' most enlightening. Howard begged to differ. "You can't sugar a bitter pill," he asserted. "If any soul mate of mine said to me, 'I understand how you feel about my infidelities, but...', then the more sincerely they intoned, the more I'd be inclined to make a pavement pizza." Louise and Howard went on to debate the issue with rising passion for some time. The others in their company, finding themselves unable to get a word in edgeways, took their leave one by one. When, finally, Louise looked at her watch, she found it to be all of two o'clock. "Well," she said, to de-escalate her way to bed, "Let's agree to respect each other's point of view, shall we? It's time to call it a day." Howard begged to differ on the last point and suggested burying the hatchet, so to speak, in his room or hers, whichever she preferred.

For a time they had lost contact, each believing their relationship to have been not so much casual as conferential. But their paths crossed again two months later. At that time, Louise was in the process of dissolving the second in the series of her marriages. She had done everything in her power to keep the lines of communication not only open but noise-free between herself and William, the other party to the formalities. However, although annulment as such was as acceptable to him as it was to her, he was driving a hard bargain where property was concerned and positively insisted on consulting a lawyer. But such sleep as Louise lost need not have been. The lawyer

William had recourse to was none other than Howard! Louise recognised his name on the first letter, one requesting her signature in agreement to an inventory of joint possessions for subsequent sundering. Uncertain that he remembered her name, or that he had even so much as once glanced at her conference badge, she called his office to reintroduce herself.

They met. Since, in the context, first, of a wine bar and, second, of Howard's apartment, their relationship could reasonably be described as personal, Louise naturally told him the whole story. Strange it is how when one tells the story of one's life, or of some more or less self-contained part of it, that things become somehow clearer, somehow more 'probable or necessary,' than they had seemed before! She honestly had not realised how many faults and shortcomings William had.

Howard was troubled. It remained his bounden duty, professionally, to do his best for his client. That went without saying. True, 'best' was a fuzzy concept, but....

Louise interrupted the decelerating train of his thought. "Why not think of it as a win-win situation?" she proposed.

"A 'win-win situation'," Howard quipped, "is better called a draw."

To do her full credit, Louise genuinely believed that life consisted in the main of win-win situations. This was by no means a simple case of calling the glass half-full rather than half-empty. It was with a certain intellectual rigour that she maintained that a win-win situation could not equally well be described as lose-lose. She had read a little around the subject and was able to retort: "*Only* if what we're dealing with is a *zero-sum game.*"

It was Howard's move. "Oddly enough," he began, "that's just how dividing up a matrimonial estate

43

appears to me. If, for example, William gets the country cottage, on the grounds that it was his before, you don't. Am I correct? Hm?"

Louise was silent. She looked down. Preferring life to be sublime, she had an understandable tendency to overlook its sordid details.

"No, there's only one thing for it," Howard continued honourably. "I'll have to fall on my sword."

As dramas made out of crises go, that seemed a little O.T.T. Suspension of disbelief was therefore less than willing. Louise communicated as much in the wide way she opened her eyes.

"I mean resign the case," he explicated.

"How would that help? He'll go to someone else."

"I'll represent you."

Louise was deeply shocked at the idea. It was against all her principles. "I just couldn't live with myself," she protested, "if I needed a *lawyer* in something as life-skills-challenging as a *divorce*."

"Then think of me as your... partner instead."

"Partner?" Louise asked, sensing an ambiguity.

"In life. And in...."

Louise was deeply touched, but saw and pointed out, before Howard had finished, a small snag.

"Mere chronology. We'll kick off," said Howard, "in medias res, then file the formalities ex post facto, leaving absolutely no bigamous mens rea to fret over. Can't you see it?" He took one of her hands. "The chemistry is there." He took the other of her hands. "I think we should legitimise our liaison *and* get into bed together business-wise. *Pre-marital divorce consultancy and contracts.* You handle the subjective, I'll handle the objective. Together, we can make sure those wires get crossed only as and when it suits us. That's what I call a *team*."

And so it was that they came now to be putting their heads together in poor Mary's case.

When, some forty minutes later, poor Mary called back as contracted, she confirmed Louise's suspicions by answering to the description of a deserted woman, for that is how Louise had framed the question.

"I can help you, Mary," Louise told her old friend. "Howard and I can both help you. Right now you're hurt, bitter, confused, ashamed. You're bereaved, bewildered, belittled. You're distraught, disorientated, disgraced. You're on the rubbish heap as a partner, unsexed as a woman and downsized as a person. I know *just* how you feel. But there's a light at the end of the tunnel. What you need is *emotional separation*. Our method is tried, tested and guaranteed to work within three months, only in your case I can't say 'or your money back' since we wouldn't dream of charging. There, I'm sure you're feeling better already."

SEVEN

Jennifer put her hand up.

'Yes, Jennifer?' Ms Pringle assented.

"Perhaps it would have been better..."

"In your opinion," Ms Pringle prompted.

"In my opinion," said Jennifer, applying the appropriate transformation rule.

"Remember, citizens of the classroom, by saying 'in my opinion' we show awareness of the existence of different points of view. That way we do not claim information-superiority, so that we are not too dominating. Go on, Jennifer."

"Well, wouldn't it have been better if Ranesh's parents, I mean her... the...."

"Let's call them her primary carers," Ms Pringle assisted. "Putting your opinion forward as a question is equally unintimidating. Good."

"Yes. Them. If they had never told Ranesh?"

"Not in *my* opinion," Ms Pringle dissented. "You see, it's all a question of fundamental human rights. Children have fundamental human rights too, you know. I'm sorry, I mean *adults-to-be*. As you all know, in *my* opinion the word 'children' is best avoided. It puts too little emphasis on the fact that you are growing up."

The re-locatable temporary structure in which future adults were being sensitised to language ought to have symbolised the transience of youth. But it had been in place at least twenty years. Hence it reflected something stuck instead.

"Aren't you going to answer Jennifer's opinion?" asked Jeremiah, a boy whose precocious, almost mid-teenage sullenness made Ms Pringle ever alert to possible corroborations of domestic abuse.

"We do not *answer* the opinions of others," Ms Pringle corrected. "Instead we *share* our own opinions with them. But before doing so, we politely suggest that they should *think more carefully* about their opinions. I shall demonstrate how. Jennifer, why don't you try putting yourself in Ranesh's position? Now, if you were Ranesh, wouldn't you want to know the truth?"

Jennifer thought this through, as carefully as she could, for a moment. "Yes. But only if I knew it already," she asserted in a qualified way, "because if I didn't know, then I wouldn't know there was something I wanted to know. Would I?"

Ms Pringle had not anticipated that the debate would take such a philosophically rigorous twist, but she reacted with unflurried professionalism. "Can anyone see what's..." – she neatly sidestepped the cruelly dismissive word which had presented itself – "what still has to be thought about more carefully in Jennifer's argument?" she asked, opting thus for a learner-centred, but suitably guided, pedagogy.

But no one could.

"I think Jennifer's right in my opinion," said Georgina, who was Jennifer's best friend and who sensed a confrontation in the offing.

"Georgina, you know you should put your hand up before speaking, don't you?" said Ms Pringle, after first smiling pleasantly. Then, satisfied that both in body language and vocal tone she had positively emphasised the positive prior knowledge held rather than the negative behaviour committed and thus had not threatened the spirited but vulnerable adult-to-be's sense of self-worth, she went on to reinforce the general principle involved. "We put our hands up before speaking not out of respect for teacher as an icon of authority. We put our hands up out of respect for the community, that is, the class. In this way we discriminate positively in favour of those who are less assertive than ourselves, Georgina."

Georgina's sense of self-worth was indeed undented. "When my mum and dad have a row," she retorted, proudly, "after a while, one, mostly it's dad, shouts 'Let's get the bloody ball out!' It's an old rubber ball. Then only the one who's holding it is allowed to speak. That way they start speaking one at a time. We could do that."

"That's a very good idea, Georgina," said Ms Pringle (while mentally noting the now evident source of the girl's confrontational style), "in situations where a married couple argue in the comfort of their own home. But it isn't necessary if they choose to hold their arguments in front of a trained mediator."

"You mean, then they have to put their hands up *too*?" asked Georgina, deeply shocked at the possible collapse of her image of adulthood.

"Not exactly, no. I mean that the mediator is trained to facilitate genuine communication and in this sense takes the place of the rubber ball. As your teacher, I too am a trained mediator. You can think of me as just like a rubber ball."

The whole class laughed, to Ms Pringle's considerable surprise. She had neglected to take into account the fact that she was seven months pregnant.

Ms Pringle smiled, directing her smile towards different parts of the classroom to broadcast the fact that, really, she was not at all embarrassed, truly. Why, she even shared the joke. Nonetheless, she sensed herself stretching upwards, holding her head as high as possible, wishing she were taller. She was in fact above average height, but the adult-to-be which still inside her, as it is inside each and every one of us, had been awakened. What good had all those counselling sessions done? What use the talking cure? The wound was still there, the wound was still open. But her father had only meant it as a joke. It was only his clumsy, *man's* way of trying to make her feel better. No, she did not blame him. Yes, she *did* blame him. He'd been drinking, as usual. He had been downright *merry*. Whenever he was merry, he joked. Jokes were a kind of violence, after all. She would always blame him. He had made it impossible for her to develop an eating disorder! A 'joke'! She was not "too fat," she was just "too short". A 'joke'! As a result, anorexia was forever ruled out as a way to get through to him.

"Now, where were we?" she said, to restore order both in the classroom and among her own thoughts. "Oh, yes. Jennifer is not sure that it was best for Ranesh to know the truth. So let's look at it another way, shall we? Put your hand up if you think you are an *individual*."

Everyone did so, including, democratically, Ms Pringle, except two identical twins. The golden opportunity this afforded her was immediately seized.

"Now put your hands up if you think Peter and Paul should have put their hands up last time."

The hands went up more tentatively this time. Ms Pringle waited before raising her own, wisely not wanting her wards to arrive at the correct answer by the educationally counterproductive means of role-model emulation. She was about to confirm the clear majority view when, oddly, she saw Paul slowly raise his hand too. Peter, however, did not.

"Paul, if you put your hand up now, it means you think you should have put your hand up before. Do you understand that?" said Ms Pringle, in a manner reminiscent of a courtroom. Her goal was to expunge all trace of reasonable doubt.

"I'm Peter," said Peter. "He's Paul."

"I told you *not* to change places. Never mind. Putting your hand up the second time but not the first means that you do not think that you are an individual, but you think that you ought to think that you are an individual. Is that correct?" The question was added so as not to have put words into Peter's mouth.

"I'm not a clone! I'm not, I'm not, I'm not!" said Peter tearfully.

"Of course you're not, dear," Ms Pringle consoled the distraught adult-to-be. But how on earth could she have used that word, with all its connotations of intimacy? How on earth could she have called Peter "dear," with its obvious invitation to him to think of her as something more than a trained mediator? How would she explain herself if the incident were reported? Would she have to confess to her own traumatic memories which had just been stirred up, to argue that this had caused her to identify with his pain, leading her into the trap of over-familiarity? But the damage had been done and Peter was still sniffing emotionally. "You're not a clone, *Peter*," (by stressing his name as a publicly acceptable term of reference she hoped that her previous lapse would be overlooked). "You're not a clone, even though your DNA is absolutely identical to Paul's, because you were made in an act of love."

"No he wasn't! His mother had to have fertility treatment," Henry called out. "My mother told me. He was fertilized in a test tube. He's a clone."

By first degree Ms Pringle was considerably more au courant with art history than biology. She therefore opted to negate Henry's claim by pointedly ignoring it. This also allowed her to jump straight to the point which she had been steadily working round to all along.

"Peter is an individual. Paul is an individual. We are all individuals," she pronounced, almost bardically.

"Being an individual does *not* mean simply having different colour eyes or hair, or a different shape nose. Being an individual does *not even* mean simply having different opinions. Being an individual means having something else. Now, citizens of the classroom, take out your vocabulary books, I want you to copy this word down.... Being an individual means having..."

In her heart of hearts, Ms Pringle had always wanted to be a dancer. Insofar as teaching involves some element of performance, it offered her the occasional opportunity to inhabit that parallel universe. Hence she turned to the board by a half-pirouette and wrote in large, bold letters: **AUTONOMY**.

She half-pirouetted back, in reverse direction, took two steps backwards to clear the general view, then gave breath to the mystical signs she had brought into being by articulating, "AUTONOMY. We are all..."

Two steps forward, another half-pirouette, but this time misjudged. The ballast of her womb carried her some thirty degrees over the one hundred and eighty intended. She retrieved the situation by completing the circle, as gracefully as her present status in this universe allowed, then asking a question instead: "Does anyone know the adjective which comes from 'autonomy'?"

"I know, I know, I know!" said Georgina, so eagerly that this time she remembered to put her hand up as soon as she had finished.

Ms Pringle turned three quarters towards the board, ready to transcribe, as a sign of sincere faith that the answer would be the desired one. By looking back over her shoulder, she gave Georgina her cue.

"*And* I know what it means," Georgina went on, realising that this time her centre-stage position had been fully sanctioned. "It means going to the pub when you want to. It's what my dad says, 'I'm an autonomous individual. I can go to the pub when I bloody well want to.'"

AUTONOMOUS appeared on the board as Georgina's glowing face looked this way and that, entitling itself to the admiration of her classmates.

"Thank you, Georgina," said Ms Pringle. Yes, the word is AUTONOMOUS. But it does *not* mean getting merry – I mean going to the pub – whenever you want to."

Georgina's face dulled. "That's what it means to my dad," she said, quietly.

Ms Pringle overrode Georgina's father with satisfaction. "Being autonomous," she expounded, "means having *personal power*."

If anyone in the classroom had been old enough, the highly charged tone with which the last two words were delivered would no doubt have reminded them of the 1960s – not the swinging version or the summer of love, but the impassioned speeches of Huey Newton, Stokely Carmichael and Angela Davies, although Ms Pringle did not actually raise her fist. And if anyone in the classroom had been old enough to be reminded of this, they would no doubt have been strangely discomfited to hear a word so lacking in the sense of collective identity as "personal" uttered in such a way.

"But *not* power without responsibility," she added.

If anyone in the classroom had been of the right demographic, the ringing absence of anything resembling passion would no doubt have reminded them of the 1980s, more precisely of Mrs Thatcher's crusade against the trade unions. But time is in the habit of moving on, leaving the better part of history initially to the confusions of the care home and ultimately to the silence of the grave. Apart, that is, from an occasional TV documentary. Indeed, Ms Pringle herself might have caught the echo from one such documentary on the miners' strike, aired but two nights before. But being in full oratorical flow, she was not listening. Nor had she finished.

"Being autonomous means having control over your own life, yes," she went on, "*but not* exercising that control in a way that reduces the autonomy of others. Does everyone understand that?" She paused, but not for long. "I'll give you an example. Georgina, if your father goes to the pub whenever he wants to, then your mother's autonomy is reduced because she has to stay at home to look after *you*."

Ms Pringle looked directly at Georgina, her eyebrows slightly raised to indicate that she expected some confirmation that her point had been taken. Georgina looked directly back. Then she raised her own eyebrows a little to indicate that, as an adult-to-be, she expected any such request to be expressed more politely. Ms Pringle looked away.

Jennifer wanted to put her hand up, but for some reason she did not. Instead, she simply said, "But what about *Ranesh*?"

"Well," said Ms Pringle, gratefully, "Ranesh's primary carers decided to tell her the truth. This was the correct decision (in my opinion) because in this way they did not *disempower* her as an individual. They did not deny her autonomy by taking a life-defining decision for her. If, instead, they had decided that it would be better for her if she did not know, they would have been treating her as... as... well, as a *child*."

"I still don't understand," said Jennifer. "How could Ranesh decide for herself that it would be better for her *not* to know something, because then she'd have to know what it was that she didn't want to know, wouldn't she?"

Ms Pringle was tired. The teaching profession was much more demanding than most people realised. Her salary was barely enough to make ends meet. It was

Friday afternoon. "Anyway," she said, "it all turned out for the best, didn't it?"

"Because it's a story," said Jennifer, in what seemed a bitter foretaste of the wisdom that comes (sometimes) with age. "In a book."

EIGHT

Jennifer's grandmother, John's mother, would have been described as a dear little old lady by any casual observer. Closer acquaintance, however, revealed her to be charming, petite, in her third age and still unambiguously feminine. As a role-model for senior citizenship, in other words, she was made, indeed self-made, rather than born. Nevertheless the sweetness of her smile contained no implication that ageism would be tolerable to her.

Her powers of recall had not been eroded by the passage of the years and in particular her short-term memory remained as sound as a bell. "That rings a bell" was in fact one of her catch phrases. However, in the way she found herself looking back more and more towards the upper reaches of all that water under the bridge which had been her life, she was no exception to the general rule; for, as the physical body approaches the open ocean of dissolution, the mind swims back upstream, like a salmon, to its place of formation, trying (quite unlike a salmon) to make sense of something.

As the past – her life, or last year, or last month, or last week – seemed in retrospect to have passed more quickly, so the present seemed to present itself ever more slowly. Days sometimes dragged. But she made herself busy. At this point in time, she was at home baking an apple pie. It was Friday, one of Jennifer's days.

'Now where *did* I leave the sugar,' thought Mary. (By pure coincidence, John's wife and mother bore the same name.) 'Let me see. I must have last used it yesterday morning, when Mrs Smith came round. Mrs Smith likes two spoonfuls in her tea, with milk, and she visits me every Thursday morning. Today is Friday. I prefer lemon, not only for reasons of diet, but taste too. Twenty years without milk, how time flies. In my tea, that is. I still enjoy it with my *Special K*. Milk. Tea. Tea. Oh yes, the sugar. After Mrs Smith left, let me see, yes, I took the sugar from the bowl and I put it back in the sugar tin. Yes, but I must have taken the tin to the bowl, not the bowl to the tin. Why ever did I do that? Let me see. Yes, I know, the bowl was still quite full and I was worried I might spill some if I tried to carry it to the kitchen and then had to answer the phone if by chance it happened to ring. Let me see. Yes, that's when the phone *did* ring, what an odd coincidence, but I didn't want to upgrade my cavity wall insulation. Or perhaps I'm becoming clairvoyant. Let me see. Then I started taking the sugar tin back to the kitchen when the phone rang again! No, I don't think I can see the future because I hadn't expected two calls. This time it was my friend, Mary, Mary Smith. Not Dolly Smith, of course, because she'd just had a cup of tea here with me. No, two cups. We talked, Mary Smith, I mean, and I, for *almost half an hour*. First we talked about the weather, how it's always so typical in late November. Then we talked about the novels we'd been reading, as usual. Hers was too predictable in its plot, although the characters were three dimensional, but mine used red herrings to very good effect. Unusual in a romance. Still, the setting was uninspiring. Colchester. But I mustn't remember all that or I'll forget what it is I'm trying to remember now. Half an hour is a long time to compare literary notes *and* to remember that something is not in the proper place. Let me see. Yes, of course, the sugar tin. So that must be it.'

She went over to the phone (which was cordless for convenience but Mary preferred to keep it continuously charged and consequently in a memorable place) and retrieved the sugar tin. The apple pie was thus duly completed and placed on the middle shelf of an oven preheated to 200 degrees.

Five minutes before the forty-five required by the pie were up, Jennifer arrived. In accordance with their custom, Mary asked her how her day at school had been.

"OK," Jennifer replied.

The grandmother in Mary was troubled. She was used to an enthusiastic narrative of between five and ten minutes and almost felt she knew Ms Pringle and the other children in the class. It must be John's departure, she realised, that was causing Jennifer to become a much more private person. The healing process would take time, so she said, "I've baked an apple pie, your favourite," to help cushion the next hour or so.

"Grandma, what's it like to have a baby?" asked Jennifer, without so much as a glimmer of ocular joy at, let alone any vocal celebration of, the prospect of the pie.

A thrill of horror passed through Mary. She steadied herself. Statistical considerations strongly suggested that this was simple, childish curiosity. "In what sense, dear?" she asked, not only to buy some time with which to breathe deeply, but also to determine more precisely what was on Jennifer's still budding mind.

"*In what sense?*" repeated Jennifer, as if she were pulling a face. This, of course, was her childish way of asking 'In what sense of what sense?'

"Do you mean to give birth or to have a baby to look after?"

"To give birth, *of course*," said Jennifer. "I said 'having a baby,' not 'having a baby *around*'. Do you love it naturally? As soon as it comes out?"

The thrill of horror had passed, as thrills usually do. Mary was back to her old self.

"But you see, darling," she pointed out, "you don't really remember that kind of pain."

"Grandma, what are you talking about?"

"Giving birth, of course. You only remember that it hurt."

"Then you do remember it."

"Yes, but there are two different kinds of pain: physical pain and emotional pain. When you remember physical pain, like a toothache, the memory doesn't hurt, does it? But when you remember emotional pain, it does."

Jennifer was not usually concerned by what seemed quite frequent lapses of concentration, or at least a tendency to lateral thinking, on her grandmother's part. For a very young person, it is difficult to realise in a fully imaginative way that a very old person has ever been anything other than a very old person. Hence a very old person appears to have been a very old person for a *very* long time. That must be very tiring.

Still, Jennifer felt fully entitled to get back to the point. "But do you love the baby naturally?" she repeated.

"Yes," said Mary. Her eyes grew misty, so she quickly went to get a cloth and a bottle of Mr Muscle and started cleaning the one window in the small living room which opened upon the damp, grey November day outside. Then, fully recovered, she turned and said, "Jennifer... do you know what contraception is?"

"*Of course*," said Jennifer. "I'm not thinking of having a baby. I was thinking about mummy. I was used to mummy not taking much notice of me before, but when daddy left I really expected her to take more interest and especially to do everything she could to help me realise that daddy leaving wasn't my fault in any way. But she doesn't. Instead she spends all day reading *What Car?* So I think I must be adopted, just like Ranesh."

"Is Ranesh a new girl?" Mary asked, for she had not heard the name before.

"She's a girl in a school story book. I know it's completely normal to be adopted," Jennifer continued, "but I don't want to be normal in that kind of way, because then I'd have to spend years and years trying to find my biological parents, without ever finding them, so that in the end I could come to terms with the fact that the people who really matter to me are my primary carers, just like Ranesh, only in my case I'm not sure that they're carers, although I suppose they are primary."

"Jennifer," Mary said incontrovertibly, "you are *not* adopted. I first met you when you were one hour old in a hospital bed beside your mother."

"You don't *meet* a baby," laughed Jennifer.

Mary was firmly convinced that you do. But she preferred to change the subject. (Jennifer would realise the truth when *she* became a grandmother.)

"*What Car?*" she said. "How long has your mother been reading *What Car??*"

"Since yesterday. *And,*" Jennifer intoned, "that was when I caught her taking a selfie – while sitting on the kitchen counter of all places!"

"Goodness," Mary reflected. "Wherever will it all lead?"

Further reflections were wisely kept to herself. 'It sounds as if Mary will tell John never to darken her door again,' Mary brooded. 'He's in out of his depth, I'm afraid, and drifting with the wind. There're no two ways about it, it's a case of sink or swim. But who dares, wins. He needs to go out on a limb if he's going to get his feet back on the ground. It's now or never and the ball's in his court, but he's not going to take the initiative off his own bat. Yes, the time is ripe for some motherly advice.'

"I'd like some apple pie," said Jennifer.

"Oh, no! I forgot the pie!" Mary cried out.

"It's *all right*," Jennifer said calmly. "I went and took it out of the oven when you were cleaning the window."

NINE

"Yes, mother, I promise I'll think it over, initial scornful laughter notwithstanding. Now hand me over to Jennifer, will you? I've only got a few minutes, as I believe I said a few minutes ago, logically putting myself in something of a spot. Jobs positively coming out of my ears, in fact. Ciao.... .... Hello, darling. How is daddy's little girl today? ... I miss you too.... Well, not this weekend, I'm afraid. The problem is, as of yesterday, mummy's no longer playing cricket. She's positively insisting on me upping the money I hand.... Yes, that's right, the *maintenance*, clever girl – though I'm sure *you* realize I'm far from being an ultra-high-net-worth individual – anyway, she's insisting on me upping that before she'll consent to – do you know what an *access agreement* is? ... I guessed you would. To an equitable one, then. I would if I could, of course, but given that the root of all evil doesn't grow on trees, daddy is without the wherewithal.... I see. So mummy's friend Louise is back, is she? ... Yes, and Louise's new husband *is* a lawyer, isn't he? ... Mmm. That does explain it, doesn't it? Maybe I should take legal counsel myself.... Do you really think so? Not mummy, surely? I've always thought of her as being, you know, see-through.... Well, not exactly like a ghost, no.... So you'd advise a cooperative conflict style, then? ... Uh huh.... Mmm.... Ah ha.... Well, daddy's little girl isn't just a pretty face, is she? That really is a cunning plan. I promise I'll think it over and I'll call you tomorrow. I've got to get my skates on now, though. I'm up to my rapidly receding hairline in paper. Still, that's being a grown up, always keeping the wolf from the door – or doors, as the case may be. You'll still be at grandma's, won't you, stopping over as per usual? ... Bye, bye, darling."

John spent the next two or three minutes thinking through Jennifer's proposal, determining the ins and outs, weighing up the pros and cons, perusing, as it were, the small print, and was just about to come to the conclusion that the end would justify the means... when suddenly he remembered the earlier suggestion which he had also pledged – initial scornful laughter notwithstanding – to think over.

Taken at face value, at first glance and on the surface, his poor deluded mother's proposition was nothing short of rearranging the deckchairs on the Titanic, with not enough method in it to qualify even as madness. And yet, for some obscure reason he could not put his finger in the general direction of, let alone upon, he was deeply disturbed to find that he could not bring himself to laugh her idea out of court, nor even dismiss it out of hand. On the contrary, when he tried to turn his thoughts once again to Jennifer's more pragmatic and practical vision, to his horror he could no longer recollect the broad outline of her strategic plan, let alone the fine detail.

He had it in him. No question of that.

Something was stirring in the recesses of his soul, a reckless impulse. It had never occurred to him before that a career-limiting move might possess such an incomprehensible, fatal allure. He was standing on the edge of a cliff (as it were), in the sense that something was pulling him forward, towards what was, at best, a leap in the dark, and at worst, a fruitless fishing expedition.

Yet deep inside he sensed a fundamental truth, that there are occasions in life when one's own better nature might be one's own worst enemy. All his life he had played safe. This was because he found it insufficiently axiomatic that fortune favours the brave, to the precise extent that bravery, apparently, remained necessary. But where had this attitude got him?

John surveyed the pied-à-terre which was now his humble abode. 'Yes,' he thought grimly, '"humble" *is* the mot juste for the furnished bedsit with kitchenette in which I now find myself. The boredom I've felt of late could well be put down to the state of that carpet. If I don't get a grip on myself it might even turn into fully-fledged ennui, what with that wallpaper.'

It didn't even pass the dead cat test.

'But would it help to think of it as a *garret*?' he mused.

He had been planning to call Angela at around this hour, having calculated that she ought to be back from Oxford. For the time being, however, he felt no great urge to do so. He sensed that he had arrived at a defining moment in his life, that he was standing at the crossroads. It was a pity, he mused on, that what he had on his professional plate generated little in the way of call of duty. The West Wimbledon Association of Residential Centres was contemplating a full public-face re-focus programme involving a raft of rebranding initiatives. (Among other things, its current motto, "Fresh Fields and Pastures New," had the unfortunate connotation of being put out to grass.) But John no longer felt he had the deadline-driven achievement-orientation necessary for such a 24/7 operation. In fact, he couldn't contemplate the thought. This was a pity because thinking about something completely beside the point is usually the best way to take a major decision, at least as a first step.

The first step, after all, is always the most difficult one.

The difficulty inherent in the first step is whether or not to take it.

But the first step sometimes takes itself, even if you don't.

Hence avoiding the issue is the best way to find out if you can't avoid the issue.

Then not taking the first step is the first step.

Who does not dare, wins.

He was losing himself. He was losing himself in his thoughts. He was losing the thread, losing track, losing time....

*   *   *

A strange noise, something like trying to start a very, very small car with a very, very flat battery, underwater, aroused John from the trance-like state into which he had fallen. The only explanation that occurred to him, as his thoughts regrouped, was that it was his doorbell, or door-something. If so, then he had his first visitor. Curiosity impelled him to the front door. Expectantly, he opened it, having not been expecting anyone.

Angela stood framed by the emptiness of the street, a sheen of drizzle on her elegant, dark blue coat. It might have been morning dew and she a flower! John had never seen her look so beautiful. Her oval face, under the thick, red hair, seemed to have a light of its own. But even as he saw this, his attention was caught by the song of a thrush. The song of a thrush in Clapham, in November, in the night. The song of a thrush, unnatured by yellow lamplight. It made John want to take Angela away with him, to take her away from all this, to save her from... he did not know what from.

"I did it."

The simplicity of her words threw him completely. "Did what?" he inquired.

"I got the job."

She was different, transformed. Not only was her tone stress-free, there was nothing of the computer animated kick boxer left in the way she held herself. Perhaps it was the warm glow of success. Perhaps, after a monumental self-marketing effort, she was just emotionally and mentally exhausted.

"Congratulations," John reciprocated. "Like a drink?" Contagiously, he too felt the need only for simple words and phrases.

They made their way down the seedy hallway, a hallway that seemed to record hundreds of similar encounters; a hallway which rendered intimacies poignantly collective and collectively unfulfilled.

"I came straight here."

Devotion was not Angela's style. John stopped, some vague sense of foreboding having been stirred by her subtext. He looked her in the eye. "Why?" he asked.

"I came to say thank you."

"So this is... goodbye?"

"No, it's thank you. Goodbye comes a little later. We're having a drink, aren't we? Which is yours?"

They entered the narrow room which answered to the possessive pronoun, where John poured two whiskies. (By reason of a recent economy drive, he had given up soda.) "To... how about to D. H. Lawrence," he proposed, raising his glass.

"No. To being oneself."

"To being oneself," John responded. "Whatever that means."

They both sat. The ensuing silence was without tension, but equally without relaxation. They were not strangers, so there was no need for polite conversation. But nor did they know each other.

Then Angela began to speak, quietly, reflectively at first, as though needing to remind herself more than to explain to him. "I just answered their questions," she said. "Lawrence didn't get a look in. I didn't have my own agenda. I was just me. You wouldn't have recognised me. And the bizarre thing is, it's thanks to you. I know you weren't trying to, but you did your job. Hence the thank you."

John had no idea, not even the faintest, what she was talking about. So he looked blank.

"When I threw you out, I said things. Remember? Spontaneous things. Unfiltered and uncensored things. Things I hadn't realised. You see, I really hadn't realised that I was trying to compensate for the fact that I've hardly seen my father in ten years by going to bed with a man I could reasonably fantasise was him." She paused. "Of course, now that I'm no longer unconscious of my unconscious desires, it's over. Finished."

"But I'm *not* your father," John pointed out.

"Exactly. That, in a nutshell, is what I realised. Hence the goodbye."

John felt deeply frustrated. To him, the de facto non-incestuous nature of their relationship was a definite plus. But how could he argue with someone who seemed so at one with her Electra complex?

He made a desperate move. "But I can give you affection," he cried. "You'll still need affection!"

"Affection?"

"Yes. Affection."

"What's that?"

"You're a woman, aren't you? In my experience, as a relationship matures, a woman starts to say 'But I only want affection,' or, often enough, 'But I only *wanted* affection'."

"But what is it?"

Confronted by such an unusual lacuna in lexical competence, many a man would be lost for words. John was not. "Well, fortunately, Mary, my wife (as was)," he said, "once gave me a complete breakdown. Affection, apparently, is a species of touching behaviour, more or less active and roving, but restricted to certain zones. But there's a subtlety involved. Not only must you restrict your hands to the affectionous zones, you – that's me, or men in general – mustn't caress them as if they're erogenous instead. You see?"

"Negative definition. How *do* you caress them?"

"Good question. I had to ask it myself. Affection, she explained, is basically what one's father or mother could administer to one physically without giving any of the caring professions, police included, cause for concern. That's the childhood paradigm. In the present context it's a transaction between consenting adults."

"It doesn't sound very exciting."

"I think that's the point, as I understand it."

"Sorry, John. Latency is not my style."

John fell silent, as though defeated. The wind of change was blowing through his private life. Angela seemed on the point of a unilateral declaration of independence or at least of voting with her feet.

Then, suddenly, something clicked. Strangely, the various unravelling threads of his life seemed to be coming together after all!

"Well, thanks for the thank you," he said, in the tone of one coming to terms with the results of a recent reality check. "I'm glad to have been of service. Really and truly. That form of words, in the context of a goodbye of this magnitude, would normally be intended to arouse guilt feelings. Not in my case. Job satisfaction, in my book, is one of life's blessings. That's not the only reason I wouldn't ask for a fee, of course. There's also the difficulty of describing it as all in a day's work.... But you could do me a favour."

Having, that very day, stepped onto the first rung of the ladder of success, Angela was in a generous mood. "What?" she said.

"Give me some advice – on and off, here and there, now and then, not necessarily on a regular basis."

"In other words..." said Angela, pointedly.

"A strictly secondary consideration. You see, it's your specialism I'd like you to share with me."

"As against my speciality?"

"Scout's honour. And phased out in the long term. Probably. We can institute the clean break then. If you like."

Negotiations to this point having taken the form of talks about talks, Angela suggested that John lay his cards on the table with one carefully chosen word.

"Well?"

"My mother's idea, bless her. She thinks I'm confused, mixed up, lost my bearings. She's my mother, after all. She wants me more to sort myself out than merely pull myself together, which requires more in the way of getting back to basics. Root and branch restructuring as to purpose in life, leading by way of affirmative action to enhanced feel-good factor with respect to self. So she won't have to worry where she went wrong – as any mother would, bless them. But how? Well, she's my mother, you see. She believes in me; in fact, after all due consideration, forty-two years worth, she still thinks my feet are most definitely not of clay, not to mention the fact that in the final analysis it's never too late, so, well, her suggestion is that I write a novel."

"Write a *what*?" said Angela, as though suffering momentary amnesia with respect to her specialism.

"I couldn't see the rationale either," John went on. "Not at first. But everyone has one novel inside them, haven't they? So what, you may well ask. True, but, well, up till now, up until this evening in fact, I thought that one step back was only ever justified if it led to two steps forward, leaving you one up. But now, in a kind of profound insight into the limitations of rational thought, or as I prefer to think of it, in something like actually hearing the sound of one hand clapping, I can see that two steps back might also be worth it, if they lead to one step forward."

"Leaving you one down," Angela computed.

"But going in the right direction," John pointed out, to transcend the merely quantitative analysis. "And...." He hesitated. "And...." He hesitated again. "I'm the *creative type*, damn it! I've got to accept it! I can't fight it! Creativity isn't just a *gift* – it's an *obligation*! I've got something to give! I've got a responsibility to the world!"

To Angela, having so recently lived through her own process of self-discovery, something in John's words seemed uncharacteristically sincere. Of course, sincerity did not rule out the possibility that he might, simultaneously, be trying to keep a foot in the door of a physically interactive relationship, even to the point where bodily fluids entered the picture. But she felt she could handle any expressions of deep frustration at having writer's block, or heart rending tales of childhood as and when stirred up, or even straightforward longing looks that he might come up with.

"A novel?" she said, returning to square one.

"Yes."

"You'd like *my* advice?"

"Yes."

"I'll do it," she announced. "But on one condition. It's your novel, of course, since it's inside you. But that's also the sense in which it's *not* a novel. A novel is a novel is a... well, for you I'll just say 'form,' but only in inverted commas. Inside you, it can't have a 'form,' obviously. That's where I come in. Since I don't want to be associated, even anonymously, with anything pre-post-modern, I'll give you advice about the 'form' on the condition that you take it. As for 'content,' or whatever you want to call it, I'll leave that entirely to you and your fantasies."

"Sounds reasonable," John acquiesced. Then, realising that this too called for a drink, he poured two more whiskies. He raised his glass.

"To... a new beginning," he proposed. He had intended this to refer to the new phase of life he was embarking upon, with a possible allusion to his relationship with Angela. But it immediately occurred to him, in these first flushes of creative energy, that it might also refer to the projected work of fiction. Hence he expanded the formula.

"In fact, to a new beginning, a new middle, and a new end."

"Oh, no!" Angela groaned. But realising that work had yet to become earnest, or even to begin, she bowed to ceremony.

"All right, but *not* in that order."

PART TWO

Everything to play for

TEN

Mary was experiencing a truly titanic struggle between emotion and reason, although one whole month had passed since her husband had moved on as an individual. When she had actually been living with John, amicably, cooperatively and under the same roof, her emotional and rational sides had enjoyed analogous relations, like a couple long grown used to each other's little ways. As John's absence had made itself fully felt, however, separation had become more than just an existential fact to be faced. It was also, by domino effect, a psycho-drama to be acted out. In a nutshell, what, in more peaceful times, had been different *sides* of herself had become, with the outbreak of hostilities between them, different *selves* – and each had an attitude.

She expressed a rough approximation of the above to Louise, one day while going for a spin down to Brighton in her new car. Her principal goal was to acquaint Louise with this enhancement of her identity, a sixth-generation Volkswagen Golf GTI, but this had been achieved at a fairly early stage of the trip.

"It's like being on a rollercoaster," she summed up. The figure of speech seemed all the more poignant in the context of such a smooth drive.

Louise was concerned. In her experience, conflict between reason and emotion had to be handled with all due care, especially when it reached proportions that could only be described mythologically. One's rational self tended to take the more objective and longer-term view of one's interests, true, but one's emotional self was not likely to take being trodden on lying down. The model she inclined to saw the emotional self as the Child within one and the rational self as the Adult within one. From this it followed that what the Child wanted was *recognition* by the Adult.

"You have to *express* your feelings," she began. "Better out than in, as some men say about something quite different but not entirely unrelated. There's such a thing as emotional detoxification too, you know. I suggest you write an email to John telling him *exactly* what you think of him. But don't send it. Print it instead so that you can tear it up, exactly as you would have done a letter in the old days."

"I don't see what good that would do," said Mary.

"Something more violent then. Print a photo of him but make sure you're not in it. Put it on a board, then throw darts at it using all the taboo language you can think of. Has to be out loud, by the way."

"I don't see what good that would do either."

"Look, you *mustn't* feel guilty at feeling anger," Louise counselled, realising that something more in the way of ritual was called for. "He must have left something behind, something personal, clothing perhaps, a tie or something. I know, one odd sock. Burn it, bury the ashes in the garden, then take a long hot bath with something from Lush."

"I think there's some misunderstanding," said Mary. "I should have been more specific. I didn't mean that my emotional self was full of rage and shame at being cast aside, let alone asunder, while my rational self was fully absorbed in coming to terms with the increase options-wise of a new other-half-free life, or anything like that. It's more a case of rationally thinking I ought to give John a second chance when he changes his mind and emotionally not being sure I want to, actually."

"I see," said Louise, somewhat irked to have been left so long barking up the wrong tree. "What misled me, I suppose, was the word 'titanic'. What you've described sounds more like a difference of opinion between two of the seven dwarfs."

Mary was silent for a moment. Then, softly, almost shyly, she added: "There's more to it".

When the unspeakable is spoken, it is usually necessary to confirm the fact.

"You haven't...?"

"Yes. I have."

"I mean, you're not...?"

"Yes. I am."

"But *how*? Sorry, I didn't mean to make it sound like, you know, something entirely out the question."

The lay-by one hundred metres or so further down the road was clearly meant to be. Mary pulled over, parked, switched off the purring engine, turned to Louise and said: "Destiny".

Louise looked at her curiously. She had never before heard Mary resort to pagan forms of belief. "I suppose he's tall, dark and handsome too," she said, hinting at some scepticism.

Mary blithely ignored the entire scientific world view implicit in that hint. "There's something bigger than we are," she testified. "We've got to be open to it. We've got to go with it. We've got to let it take us where it will."

"Well, tall, dark and handsome or not, he sounds like a good fuck."

Whenever in the past (that is, in Mary's other life) Louise had had recourse to the f-word, even (as on this occasion) in the best possible taste, Mary had betrayed some embarrassment by looking away or clearing her throat or making some marginal improvement to the propriety of her dress. Not this time. She looked Louise squarely in the face, smiled radiantly and said with girlish, but far from tongue-tied, simplicity, "Yes".

Girl-talk having thus been firmly broached, Mary went on to try to define the precise differences between Ron's (for Ron was as she now knew the AA man) and John's emotional largesse, staying power, and sensitivity to what she as a woman really wanted. Finally, after weighing the significance of the smallest detail, she found a satisfactory formula.

"John saw me as... as like a computer program. Input all his, output all mine. But Ron...."

She started the car, unthinkingly. It purred, as narcissistically as any cat, to draw attention to its sleekness of line.

"Ron sees me as having... as having *horsepower of my own!*"

She revved the engine. The purr rose to a roar in promise of power, yet somehow remained a purr in amplitude. Dangerous but responsive. Thrilling yet soothing. Her hand reached for the handbrake. She released it easily, as though slipping into something more comfortable. Words had become inadequate, redundant, superfluous. The speed with which Mary went from 0 to 60 told Louise *everything!*

*   *   *

Objectively, as classified in the trade press, Mary's new Golf was an image and financial compromise, but subjectively there had been no doubt in her mind once she had first set prospective buyer's eyes upon the legendary model. She understood at once why it had been Europe's biggest selling car, even before the test drive. The salesman explained to her that although the Golf was clunkier in the gear-shift and grabbier in the brakes than, for example, the Ford Focus, the lightness of the steering made the driving experience almost ethereal. Not only that, but generous fore-aft seat movement, driver's height adjustability and in-out, up-down configurability of the steering column, not to mention Adaptive Chassis Control (optional) amounted to nothing less than complete customisation where user-friendliness was concerned. Two litres was generally recommended for a young and attractive woman, but would she prefer automatic or manual transmission? Mary wasn't sure. What did the different levers actually look like? He showed her. After that, Mary never again thought of the word "manual" as being essentially negative in connotation.

Out on the Wandsworth Road for a test drive it was relatively difficult to experience the transports of delight associated with fourth, fifth or sixth gears, but the salesman beside her drew her attention to the various creature comforts which made stop-start driving a pleasure in itself. He then asked how she found the excellent all-round visibility. "Excellent," she replied. "Yes," he said, "our lady customers are generally more discriminating than is the average man. All he thinks about is performance. We do our best to educate them, but it's like showing a bunch of Millwall supporters round the Turner Prize Show. Selling to ladies like yourself, on the other hand, that's what makes this job worthwhile. A woman, as I see it, is a more complex creature than a man. She has a wider range of moods. Some of my colleagues hold the theory that ideally she'd have a different car for each and every mood. But I don't agree. I point out that then she'd often be late for an important appointment on account of not having been able to choose which car to go in. No, as I see it, she needs a car which adapts itself to every mood, a car in and through which she can put career first, be sexual dynamite *and* a good mother as and when required. And you're driving it."

In due course the purchase was arranged and Mary took ownership of her new car. In more technical terms the vehicle was 'used' as against 'new,' but Mary persisted in a kind of denial of its full service history, no doubt because of the role she felt sure it would play in an all-round renewal of the meaning of life. Nor, strictly speaking, was it 'owned' in the full statutory sense, such as would have obtained had she had sufficient cash in hand or even at hand in the bank. Here, however, she persisted in the primitive belief that possession is nine tenths of the law, a maxim which self-evidently pre-dates the age of credit.

A variety of stimuli had led her to the revolutionary response of getting her own car, which was by no means to be explained in terms of throwing caution to the wind or leaping before she looked. As a shot, it had not been taken in half-light, let alone the dark. In the first place, the forty-five minutes between Louise first phoning and Mary phoning back, on that fateful Wednesday afternoon in latish November, had not been occupied in their entirety atop the kitchen units. She and the AA man had managed to squeeze in a good ten minutes further conversation. During this, he had briefly inquired whether she and her husband had any plans to replace their old Volvo – with something no longer straight off the production line, to get down to brass tacks, because if so he would gladly give it a thorough going over.

Still, at this stage the possibility was of merely theoretical interest. She had inadequate purchasing power.

In the second place, Louise had explained to her over the phone that the first, major and essential step to independence was 'emotional separation'. Although the theory of emotional separation was anathema to Mary, suddenly the practice of independence no longer seemed self-evidently undesirable – in other words, isolated and alone. Still, she chose to ignore Louise's cryptic observation that, "once shot of John," she'd "trip the light fandango" (roughly translated, she would have a self-authentication and self-validation ball). "Yes," she had said pointedly. "But what about you know what?" Louise then put Howard on the line. Without the slightest ado he had asked her the most intimate of questions, comparative stranger though he was, but because he had asked it in the bluntest possible terms, she had taken his interest to be other than salacious and answered. He laughed. Then he told her she was entitled to *considerably* more than that and gave her back to Louise.

"But Louise," said Mary, "how can I *be* independent if I don't feel independent, and how can I feel independent if I'm using John's money to *be* independent?"

Mary's cavalier use of "be," with its glaring failure to discriminate between existence and essence, did not trouble Louise. "What makes you refer to it as John's money?" she responded. "It's a return on an investment."

For some time after, Mary tried to think it so. She even, up to a point, wanted to effect the paradigm shift. But there was the small matter of long social conditioning to be overcome. She was a family-person, as against a first person-person. She was other-oriented. With a significant other, above all, she was unreservedly altruistic, even in the sense of unreciprocally. In fact, she would no doubt have soon come to the conclusion that she should forget about the whole thing had it not been for the event which came in the third place.

She heard something penetrating her letter box. The scraping-rustle of paper suggested a considerable and sustained thrust. It must be sizable, to say the least, since her epistolary aperture was far from niggardly. Then it dropped with a richly portentous thud on the carpet.

On investigation, she found that it was a copy of the current issue of *What Car?* At first, she thought it must be a mistake, albeit quite a coincidence. But then she saw a thick thumbprint on the front cover – a thumbprint formed in oil!

Just as a single straw may break a camel's back (when added to a large number of other straws), so an apparently minor, insignificant event may tip the balance between one life and another. Had that glossy, gleaming, radiating magazine never lain there, like some stoned angel of annunciation, mutely asking to be picked up and thumbed through, the whole course of Mary's life might well have turned out differently. No doubt Jennifer would have been right. She would have been right when she proposed to her father that he should pay the extra maintenance requested. She would have been right in believing that her mother would feel conscience-stricken as soon as the extra disposal income was hers for the disposing. She would have been right that Mary would have soon retracted, unable to cope with the negative impact on her low self-esteem of a moment of self-assertion. But Jennifer was insufficiently aware of the Faustian bargain into which her mother had entered by opening the forbidden book. Her soul – or her long social conditioning, which is much the same thing – was lost in the moment that she stooped to pick it up.

ELEVEN

In the twenty-four days that had passed since the inglorious Milton in him had ceased to be mute, John's learning curve as a wordsmith had paralleled the uphill struggle of finding a voice. This at least meant it had gone in the right direction. He had soon discovered that the acid test for a novelist lay in delivering the goods, but often found himself staring at a virgin virtual page, clueless how to call down the muse and not entirely convinced of her ongoing immortality. On one notable occasion, nevertheless, inspiration had visited to challenge his keyboard skills to their limits. Then it was that he experienced himself not as artificer but as medium; an alternative world had seemed to realise itself without aforethought, premeditation or design, merely passing through the untended country station of his imagination like an intercity train. Then it was that he discovered what only the novelist – the *true* novelist – knows; that one's characters have a life of their own! They may lack flesh and blood, they may not breathe this earthly air, but, strange to relate, they have *wills*, wills not lent them but their very own. The novelist – the *true* novelist – must work with, not against, this mystery. He must let the offspring of his soul go where they would go, do what they would do, say what they would say – at least up to a point.

But a harder lesson was in store. It was not that the heady wine of inspiration is generally watered down with perspiration, to the point where, most days, it might as well be a non-alcoholic beverage. John had heard that this went with the territory. Rather, it was that intoxication, when it does happen and whatever its efficient cause, always gives way to a morning after and, withal, a heavy dose of the cold light of day. Reading through his MS, John discovered the other side of the creativity coin. The novelist – the *true* novelist – is his own harshest critic. He was struck by the fact that what had seemed, in the ecstasy of quasi-shamanic possession, so vibrant with pulsating truth to life, so awash with the varied colours of absolutely authentic experience, so rich with profound insights into the darkest recesses of the human soul, now seemed flat, dull and, worst of all, old hat. 'I'm supposed to be writing a novel,' John reminded himself, 'and a novel is supposed to be original. New. Novel, even. But this is all clichés. Not to put too fine a point upon it, it's ridden with clichés. On every level – plot, character, dialogue – the clichés aren't just legion; they're too numerous to mention! In the way of deathless prose,' he summed up dispiritedly, 'it's hardly the best thing since sliced bread.'

Still, tomorrow is another day, as John discovered for himself after sleeping on his sense of failure. On re-reading his text, it occurred to him that his very familiarity with what he had read yesterday (it being he who had written it) had bred the contempt he had felt. Now, with a little more distance, he felt that after all his opus had a certain indefinable something, a certain il ne savait quoi. Thus the crisis passed and with it the negative thoughts and feelings. The problem, he reflected constructively, was that its depths were hidden ones. In that light, it was not strictly a problem at all. Moreover, he pointed out to himself, the predictability of his plot was not in violation of the widely accepted (albeit strange) truth that truth is stranger than fiction. It was a good example of the power of positive thinking.

In any case, he had yet to run the first fruits of his labours past Angela. Now, twenty-four days on and three chapters in, and sufficiently satisfied with work in progress to be unsatisfied with the prospect of pressing on regardless, or rather alone, he deemed the time ripe. Unfortunately, Angela had decided to do the honourable thing and spend Christmas with her mother in Winchester, for the first time in six years, as though this was somehow in her new job description.

So he imagined her reaction instead....

Angela finished reading, seemed to ponder for a few moments, as though waking from but trying to hold on to some richly sensuous dream, then turned to look at him with eyes wide with admiration and rekindled, deepened love.

"Well?" John asked modestly.

"I'm going to have to redefine my theoretical parameters," she said huskily. "It's.... I don't know what to say."

"Don't say anything," John said generously. "Kiss me."

Their love making was intense and wild, as it had been in the beginning, but for the first time he did not feel coaxed, guided, spurred on and reined in by turns, such that he had a vague post-coital recollection of having managed a clear round. Instead, Angela seemed to want him to run wild, to offer herself to his unbridled lust. Her orgasms came thicker, faster, deeper, louder than ever before until, in the end, almost fainting, she appealed to him, appealed with fervent finger nails, with thrusting tongue, with levitating lower torso, to yield his seed unto her womb.

"You know something?" she said, when her inarticulacy had sufficiently worn off. "You are an amazingly good *read*."

'Obviously writing fiction is good for me,' John reflected. 'That's the best sex I've ever imagined.'

Professionally, as an image consultant, John's work in life could be described as the construction of fictions within the real world. Now, having found his métier as a novelist, he could be thought of as unveiling deeper realities within a fictional world. In all probability he would have gone on to ask 'What, then, is reality?' or at least to notice that it was a good question, had it not been for the fact that his most recent imaginings were erotic. They might find their way into, even form the core of, his next chapter, but for the time being they left him feeling dissatisfied with the work in hand.

No doubt it was such dissatisfaction which caused him there and then to look at his phone, as though wishing away time itself, or at least that the actuality of the present should make way for the potentiality of the future, a.s.a.p. Fortunately, be it said. For what he saw there caused him immediately to think of something completely different, as was indicated by the following exclamation:

"Oh, my God! What day is it? It can't be! Yes, it is! Oh, *Christ!*"

*   *   *

The festive season had reached its peak.

Outside, everything and everywhere was quiet. The few cars that passed and the fewer individuals who walked their dogs only drew the more attention to a pervasive, otherworldly calm – a calm entirely pure, before no storm. Somehow one knew, it was like this throughout London, throughout the South East, into the Midlands, the West Country, even the North, the same suspension of workaday life, its elevation to a higher plane. And everywhere the silence seemed to whisper the same spiritual secret in the same magic words: homo economicus is not all that we are;

consumption can exist for its own sake, disengaged from production.

True, a great productive, not to mention distributional and retail, effort is required to build to this sublime moment. But that, like a space shuttle's launch rocket, exists in order to be left behind. Or think of a man, shall we say in some Polynesian tribe, who puts on a mask. What is he? To an outsider, he is a man wearing a mask. To an insider, on the other hand, he is no longer himself, but one possessed by the spirit in the mask. The subtlety is this: the insider continues to know *who it is* who is no longer himself, but does not actually think of him as, shall we say, my friend Nanambuki. It is just the same with the English Christmas.

Yet there are many who say that The Christmas Experience has lost its meaning. Poor benighted nay-sayers, they fail to understand: Mammon is mocked by the credit card, not praised. Did not Our Lord say, "Take therefore no thought for the morrow: for the morrow shall take thought for the things of itself"? And consider a man who prays in the market place, that others may witness his piety. Truly, he prays not. But walk through the streets on December 25th, in England. Conspicuous consumption is conspicuous only by its absence.

Still, fortunately England is an advanced post-industrial society and is not commonly visited by anthropologists from Borneo. Fortunately, that is, for any such anthropologist. Had one been conducting his researches on this day, the principal feast day of the calendar, he would have been wise to bring sandwiches, or the address of a Salvation Army soup kitchen.

John marched on purposefully. Oddly enough, on this one day of the year, he might have strolled rather than strode, such was the pervasive sense of peace.

Provided he strolled with *some* residual sense of purpose, he would probably not have seemed to the Neighbourhood Watch or on CCTV to have been loitering with intent. But he was on the late side.

Mary, John's mother, looked at her kitchen clock. She was engaged in cooking a sumptuous repast with the help of Mary, John's wife (as was). She had taken upon herself the onerous task of hosting the family occasion and, withal, of laying the festive board, small though her maisonette was (it pushed the 'ette' to the limit, in fact), as part of her plan that John, as Jennifer's father, and Mary, as Jennifer's mother, should both be present for at least the most special part of this most special day, for the sake of the child, who would of course also be in attendance.

"John's on the late side," she observed.

"He's never missed Christmas before," the other replied. At once she realised her mistake. "But then...," she added, admitting this.

Mary smiled at her with deep compassion. She had anticipated that Christmas Day would be difficult for Mary. She had fully expected Mary to experience the odd visitation from the Ghost of Christmas Past.

At that precise moment, Jennifer took a short break from *The Wizard of Oz* by putting her head through the kitchen door. "Daddy'll be here in ten minutes," she announced.

"Jennifer!"

"What?"

"Come back here!"

"You come here!"

"I'm busy!"

"And I'm engrossed! It's not so easy to stop being engrossed as it is to stop being busy!"

Her mother submitted and came there. "How do you know daddy will be here in ten minutes?"

"I texted him!"

"I bought her a mobile for Christmas," Mary explained on her return to the kitchen, while stirring the Safeway Chilean Claret Enriched Demi-Glace Sauce in the recommended figure of eight motion, using a real wooden spoon.

"Isn't she rather *old* for a mobile?" Mary asked, while deftly chopping Fresh New Zealand Chives into 3mm lengths with a perfectly weighted French chef's knife wherewith to enliven Tesco Low Fat Strained Greek Yoghurt – the which was destined deliciously to dress Selected Pre-Washed Brittany Potatoes baked in foil.

"Don't you mean *young*? I think the Waitrose Bavarian Preservative-Free Hogs' Offal Sausages should be about done."

"No, I don't think so – *old*. Did she actually *ask* for it? Yes, done to a turn."

"Over and over again. I caved in to pester power. All her friends renew theirs yearly. Did you add the Transylvanian Sun-Dried Chestnuts to the Fifty Percent Organic Lincolnshire Brussels Sprouts, by the way? And, after all, both Ofcom and the Advertising Standards Authority have no teeth to speak of. You can't blame the younger consumer for full spectrum style-consciousness."

"But where will she put it? Yes I did, after soaking them overnight in milk which I'd heated but not boiled with six whole black peppercorns and a bay leaf. Are you sure the sprouts were fully fresh? They weren't in a sealed plastic bag. You did say the turkey was *self*-basting, didn't you?"

"Ethical consumerism, real re-cycled paper bags, support for small traders (at least if by chance I happen to stumble across one) – you know me. Yes. Several times, in fact. I think she'll tend to carry it with her. It's from Marks and Spencers, after all. I'm not sure about *this* recipe. The turkey, not the mobile. It suggests a little curry powder in the bread sauce."

"Mild Madras or Sainsbury's Authentic Two In One Far Eastern? It's ideal for both Thai and Malaysian dishes. I don't know, somehow I feel *inadequate* not basting it myself, but then I grew up before second-wave feminism. How much exactly?"

"Forty nine pounds, ninety nine. Low end. It's more bright, you see, than smar..."

"I mean how much curry? Goodness, I thought inflation had been under control for at least the last decade. Apart from the property market, of course."

"Um... a soupçon."

"A soupçon is half a pinch in English, isn't it? Still, I expect it's very pretty. Well, that rules out the Sainsbury's."

"Why?"

"It's in paste form. But then how will it, you know, *go round*?"

"What?"

"If she's carrying it with her, how will it actually *work*... as a *mobile*?"

"Oh hell, it's *already* time to caramelise the shallots. Oh, and plunge the tender young broccoli spears into ice-cold water, would you, to preserve their succulent Winsor green, otherwise the Valencia orange slices will look terribly out of place. I'll stuff the mushrooms with tahini, pine kernels, finely chopped Andalusian black olives and soy sauce aged in an untreated oak cask. Here's some I prepared earlier. It has a *battery*, of course!"

"Ice cubes, ice cubes. We've forgotten the garlic bread! It's still in the freezer. A *battery*! Whatever next!"

"Oh no! You really do need a microwave!"

"Never mind, never mind! I'll have to ask her myself, but I don't want to embarrass her. Perhaps it's regression after John left. Poor thing, she must be feeling insecure. How long should a Hunter Valley Shiraz breathe? It wouldn't go with cranberry sauce anyway."

"Of course it would! Look here. 'Apart from the rich blackberry follow through, once you get past the hint of sweaty saddle, this Hunter Valley Shiraz is renowned for its peppery explosion on the tongue'! It's obviously *ideal*!"

"I was referring to the garlic bread."

"*Forget* the garlic bread! The Robertson's Luxury Plum Pudding! We should have put it in the Tefal pressure cooker *six minutes ago*!"

"Well, we'll just have to spend one hour and thirty-*six* minutes on the main course, won't we? It could be a fad. I never got the hang of the hula hoop myself, even though I was still well under twenty. Where on earth is John? It's a good thing I got up at 5.30 this morning to lay the table."

On cue, albeit on the late side, John appeared in the kitchen, having been admitted by Jennifer. "Mmm! Something smells good," he said in a tone that went far beyond the call of duty. "A foretaste of delights in store. I trust this Able-Bodied Bulgarian Plonk will add something to the gastronomic extravaganza. Happy Christmas, one and all."

Mary turned slowly to face him. His eyes met hers for a moment, then... descended. She felt awkward, embarrassed. She was wearing an apron! But she had not intended to assume such familiarity! She had not intended to project any residual identity as a housewife! She had simply wanted to keep her clothes clean. The apron was, in fact, a present from his mother. But how could she tell him that? It would only compound the problem. He would see it as a female conspiracy! Instinctively, she thought of taking it off. But how would actual divestment appear to him? He would see everything – how it needed only the *gentlest* tug to unfasten the bow behind, how her hair would be ruffled just a little, if only a soupçon (but that would be worse) by the neck strap, no matter how tactfully she raised it.

The Mary on John's side of the family moved quickly to break the ice, by reciprocally wishing her son a happy Christmas.

"Yes, happy Christmas," her homonymous co-slave to the stove added, thereby completing the round.

"Well, what with one, two, three, four saucepans, one grill, one oven and UK Power Networks all at the limit of their capacity, the thought occurs that if one can't stand the heat, one had better keep out of the kitchen," John observed wittily. "Hence I'll go and park in front of the TV with Jennifer. One never tires of the classics."

(The reader may perhaps have been disconcerted by the absence of any reference to exchange of presents, occasioned by John's entrance. To clarify: John had arranged with his mother years before that mutual exchange was at best a redundant and at worst an inefficient means of maximising utility and should be discontinued, and it had not occurred to him to buy one for Mary as an *ex*-partner. As for the chocolates purchased by Mary in Chapter 3, she had eaten them in a moment of desolation.)

Mary and Mary committed once more to their high-volume culinary enterprise, but now with total task-focus under pressure. They spoke, that is, of nothing other than petits pois garnished with whole mint leaves, cleanliness retrieval of in-service implements, the requisite thermodynamic energy of presentational crockery, and such like, and that in terms succinct, to the point and unclouded by the emotional highs and lows of haute cuisine. Each remained as alert as a traffic lights fire-eating juggler to the key operational parameters of precision, safety and client satisfaction. No shortage of work surface, bluntness of utensil or even accidental spillage was outside their bandwidth! What a tragedy for the nation that no one was there to observe and learn from them! Top executives, heart surgeons, generals in war rooms, all would have gained far more from a passive presence in the kitchen of number 45, Montgomery Gardens, SW19, than from any number of Interactive Weekend Challenges in country mansions, although it was rather small.

At length the announcement came that dinner was about to be served. All hands were required to effect this, that the gastronomic analogy with the heat death of the universe might be minimised – for the meal thus served was indeed a universe in itself!

"Mmmmmmmm," said John, upon having sat down. "Jennifer?"

"Mmmmm," Jennifer seconded.

Eating then began in earnest, with nothing to speak of in the way of conversation other than compliments to the chefs, for the next ten minutes. As the tempo of indulgence slowed, however, dialogue became less contingent. This happened quite gradually. For example:

"We've missed the Queen," said John's mother.

"I'd rather say the Queen's missed us, what with a feast like this!" said John.

Later still, more heterogeneous, even food-free, remarks were made and the dinner table exchanges began to exhibit the mind's celebrated capacity to range, soar and even think.

Jennifer's grandmother inquired about her mobile. This was proudly produced and displayed. Mary then asked Mary why she had not said it was a cell phone. This stirred the patriot in John who pointed out that, well made though most American movies were, a constant diet appeared to have negatively impacted his mother's mother tongue. The defendant responded that several decades earlier she had felt exactly the same way about films. The term moving pictures had been acceptable, but she had not been reduced to speaking of movies until the special relationship between Margaret Thatcher and Ronald Reagan. John parried with the argument that Americanisms were unexceptionable, even welcome, if they were consistent with existing native linguistic forms, and that the Bulgarian was not bad, not bad at all. Movie was – unexceptionable, that is – because movement had much the same sense on both sides of the pond. Cell phone on the other hand was not, since on first coming across the term one would naturally think of an up-market prison. Moreover, in some cases the indigenous British term was to be preferred because it was more to the point. What was important about a mobile phone was the fact that one could use it on the move. True, the cell or battery (as we say) made this possible, but was surely secondary to this primary feature. His mother's succinct counter argument was to point out that we use cars, don't we?

The younger Mary looked down.

"Speaking personally," said John, "no."

Unaware of her faux pas, Mary the elder clarified that she had meant "we" in a general sense. The logic of John's position, she had meant to imply, was that we should use automobiles.

"By the way," John addressed his prototype spouse, "how are you finding it? Handling OK? Nippy enough?"

"Fine."

"Good. Good. How're the brakes?"

"Fine."

"Report has it that you have to step on them a bit."

"Yes, you do."

"But they work?"

"Oh, yes."

"Good. Good. Of course they work. I meant work well. Even though you do have to step on them."

"Yes, they do... work well."

"Good. Far from being a drawback, you could say it makes you feel more *in control*. Couldn't you?"

At this point, however, Mary senior spoke up. It was not that she felt any need to retrieve the situation. It was more a belated case of carpe diem. "Well, John," she said meaningfully, "I see you've become very interested in *words* lately."

John leaned a little back in his chair, one hand lightly grasping the stem of his wine glass which rested still upon the table. It was the posture of a satisfied man, the posture of one who might have been about to say, 'One day, all this will be yours, my boy'. In fact, if the word 'boy' were replaced by the word 'public,' the phrase would have served well enough.

"Yes, indeed. As against horseless carriages. Quite so. I have discovered, in point of fact, that one can really *go places* by means of words, yes. Off-road, and not just in the four by four sense. Metaphorically, of course, but that's not to be sneezed at, you know. Words are not just work-horses. Think, rather, of Pegasus. I, for one, wouldn't look *him* in the mouth."

"What *are* you talking about, daddy?"

"Solitude, midnight oil, long hours of travail, bouts of melancholy, the odd dark night of the soul, but at the end of the day a deep personal satisfaction. Mere material things are not what matter, darling. Man does not live by bread alone. Before too long, who knows, I may wend my way to the pawn shop – that's p-a-w-n, by the way – but with the satisfaction of knowing that I, at least, answered the call when it came."

"Do you understand, mummy?"

"I'm afraid not."

"Is it the wine talking?"

"That's not for me to say. Any more."

"I think *I* know," said the grandmother, with the kind of smile that not so much insinuates as broadcasts a knowledge claim. "Tell them, John."

"It was your idea, mother. The floor is yours."

"It's her maisonette," Jennifer pointed out.

"I mean that, as my mother and my muse, she shall be the one to reveal all."

"Well, it *is* rather warm," said Mary, winking exaggeratedly at her granddaughter. "But I think I'd rather tell them about you writing a novel."

"A novel!" exclaimed Jennifer. Her excitement was such that she felt the need to test its grounds. "Not just a story book?"

"Well," said John modestly, "it's not *nineteenth century* word count-wise. With the pace of life as it is, one naturally goes for the terse and economical. And, of course, one ought to have film rights in mind from the start. That way, dead wood tends to rule itself out. But yes, a novel *in conception*."

"What's it called? What's it called?" The eager repetition of the question seemed, oddly, to follow from the reference to conception, in the sense that it might have betrayed the desire of a hitherto only child to introduce herself to a new member of the family – but only if a psychologist had been present.

"Of course, it's not finished *yet*," the author hedged. "And you should bear in mind that there are two basic kinds of novelist: those who think of their titles *last*, often with great difficulty, and those who think of their titles *first*, often inspirationally or without knowing why. To be quite frank, open and above board, I am of the latter mould. I have found that having a title in mind serves as a light shining in darkness, or navigational beacon. Some novelists prefer detailed pre-plotting, but this, I confess, cramps my style. The result is wooden prose – not leaden, I hasten to add. It remains within the bounds of possibility that I *may* have second thoughts, at a later date, but, for the moment, my *working* title is one that, well, I'm rather fond of."

"But what's it *called*?" Even a psychologist would have understood the desire behind this further repetition of the question.

"*The Worm That Turned.*"

Silence.

"Of course, the characters are not actually from among the lesser species. They are fully human, though I say so myself. The title is a play on words."

"Well, I look forward to reading it," said Jennifer politely. "Can I pull a cracker?"

"Yes, darling," John's mother consented, as hostess. "I think it's... it's... quite... what's the word? You know, little dogs, horrible creatures. Not yappy. More aggressive." *Snap* went the cracker. "Quite *snappy*, that's it. What do *you* think, Mary?"

Mary did not know what to say. A frisson of fear, a moment's indecision between fight or flight, had been her initial or gut reaction to John's announcement. For a moment she had not understood why. Then it came back to her, vividly. She saw an inn sign, a large brown worm doubled back on itself in a field of longish green grass. She heard Ron's words: "Not long after, he murdered his wife"!

"I don't know what to say," she said. "It's... it's...". Unlike Angela, she didn't have any theoretical parameters to redefine, at least where narrative fiction was concerned. "It doesn't sound as though it's going to have a happy ending," she said instead.

"Of course it will," the older Mary said reassuringly. "Won't it, dear?"

"Ah, that would be telling."

"I don't get this joke," said Jennifer. "It says 'What's the difference between suicide and death by misadventure?' And the answer is, 'If you don't use a condom, there isn't one.' What's funny about *that*?"

"I think that's taking the Aids Awareness Campaign a bit far," John observed with a professional air. "Where did you get those crackers, mother? You see, Jennifer, you have to read 'misadventure' as *Miss Adventure*, as against its usual sense of having an *accident*. 'Miss Adventure' implies a new se... romantic partner, as seen from the male point of view, whose previous se... romantic history is far from being an open book. The point is that un-safe se... ro... sex in such circumstances is unsafe. To say the least. Something like driving a car with no brakes... for example."

Now she understood! His far too easy acceptance of her new car, his uncharacteristic insouciance over money matters, it all fell into place! It was all affected! Man does not live by bread alone, indeed! And he had referred to *her brakes* several times! Was it possible he knew about Ron? She had to think quickly. No, she would *not* raise the subject of that pub. She would *not* play his game by letting him know she knew. She would... serve the pudding.

There is only one potential trouble with getting too much of a good thing, that the more one gets *too much* of it, the less *good* as a thing it may seem. This might be supposed to apply to food, if not to all good things. Nonetheless a mediated relation complicates even this relatively straightforward case. The *too much* factor is registered first around the waist, rising by degrees through the upper intestinal region even to the stomach itself, while the *good* factor remains unaffected at the level of the palette. Add to this the fact that we all carry with us an infantile imprint of the enormity of the mother's breast, or at least of the bottle, and small wonder is it that the conventional first world option of living to eat, as against eating to live, is itself transcended, to be replaced by something like eating to attain the oceanic feeling.

Even so, nobody could possibly manage any pudding.

TWELVE

As any true novelist knows, this world in which we go about our daily business is not the only one with a cast iron claim to actuality. That readers may suspend their disbelief, authors have to go ahead of them, like explorers, encountering sometimes hostile natives, or at least characters with wills of their own, following long rivers, or plot lines, to their sources, or rather their dénouements, documenting a flora and a fauna never before beheld by mortal man. A good novel is discovered, not invented. But *where* is it discovered? Within, of course. The great paradox of writing is that to write something new we must write what we know. This is not a piece of cake.

A mere two days after Christmas, John felt the time had come to put his best foot forwards and resume the marathon task. For some time, however, he felt as though he was merely twiddling his thumbs, mentally, or contemplating his navel rather than his novel. Concentration, in other words, had been in short supply. But now, as the early evening drew on, he felt the affairs of the world receding and his characters coming back to life. The speed of his fingers quickened to all systems go as the phrases became more felicitous and the creative tension in his neck and shoulders increased to an extent he would certainly have to live with later.

How irritated he was therefore when his door-buzzer or door-squeaker or whatever it was sounded. Just how inopportune can a moment get! The sound for which there was no name sounded again, as insistently as it was able. But he was in the middle of a sentence! It too insisted – on being finished: "... when the doorbell rang," he wrote. In fact he had not been quite sure how to finish that sentence. It was Raymond Chandler who had advised: "when in doubt, have a man come through the door with a gun in his hand". Whoever was at his door, though unexpected and at an unappointed hour, had been 'on time' in a sense. Then, noting to himself that everything is grist to the writer's mill, he headed towards the front door.

Life sometimes imitates art, as art imitates life; in spite of the fact that he had more or less made the transition back to the real world, John kept himself partly shielded by the door as he opened it.

"Oh. Louise.... Hello."

"Yes, it is a surprise, isn't it?" annotated Louise.

"Well, you'd be the last person I was expecting, if it wasn't for the fact that I wasn't expecting anyone."

"Even so," said Louise, "I didn't come here just to pop by. I came to come in."

"Be my guest."

John extended his left arm in the direction in which coming in could be effected and Louise duly became his guest.

"Time for a quick one?" John asked, once inside his residence.

"Time for a slow one."

Louise sat down. In the one armchair.

"I see. Well, a question comes to mind," he said, pouring two whiskies. "To what do I owe this unexpected... honour?"

"Pleasure."

"I owe it to pleasure?"

"The phrase is 'unexpected pleasure'."

"I'd rather say that you honour me with your presence than that you..."

"Quite. It's bad for the neck, you know. After 6 pm."

"I'm sorry?"

"Don't be. Just save, close and put painlessly to sleep."

"Ah." John did so. It would have been too churlish not to.

"Must be the celebrated novel," Louise went on. *The Worm that Turned.* Interesting title. What made you choose it?"

Famous already. Mary must have been talking, anyway.

"Not sure, really. Something just drew me to it. Commercial considerations perhaps. I mean, when you're browsing through the shelves of your friendly local bookstore, what's the first thing you notice about a novel? Other than the fact that it's one of many."

"Yes, it might lure me on to the back cover, I suppose," Louise agreed. "What kind of novel is it? Romance, thriller, murder mystery?"

"More an exploration of human relationships. Not genre-specific."

"The central character, I suppose, is the worm?"

"You'll have to read it. When it's finished."

That line of inquiry appeared to have been closed. Quickly grasping this, Louise took another tack.

"What a pity you couldn't make it to my wedding-do. But what a stroke of luck your accident happened just outside a pub. Of course, that's my neck of the woods, so I'm familiarish with it. Not *so* familiar as to have actually seen the ghost though. Did you know it was haunted?"

John was perplexed. He still did not know to what he owed this honour. Or this pleasure. He felt quietly confident that Louise disliked him. She had made that patently obvious at every opportunity. Even Mary saw it. He contemplated coming right out with it and asking just what had brought her there. Of course, this would involve some tacit acknowledgement that he knew of her dislike for him. But why not? In the way she had made this obvious enough, he was clearly meant to know of it. But some approximation to natural politeness got the better of him.

"To tell you the truth, Louise, that whole incident is all still a bit hazy."

"It's not true that I don't like you, you know."

John was even more perplexed. Had he been thinking aloud?

"What gives you that idea? That I have that idea?"

"If you didn't, I'd take it as an insult. You couldn't have been taking any notice of me."

All things come to he who waits. But John had not been waiting.

"But... what made you say it now?"

"Your question."

"What question?"

"To what do you owe this... pleasure?"

"I said honour. You said pleasure."

"So I did." Louise's tone was not exactly that of one who stands corrected, more that of Edith Piaf regretting nothing.

By now, John was beginning to get the message. But there were a few outstanding details to clear up.

"But... my novel.... The... that... the name's on the tip of my tongue, damn it, you know, that pub? All that came *after* my question, as far as I recall, not to say *before* your answer."

"Small talk. I was hoping you'd come straight out with it, ask me what had brought me here, even be upfront about how patently obvious I've made my dislike of you, so I could put the record straight. But you're so unnaturally polite. In the end, I decided to take the initiative... or more to the point, the bull by the horns."

"But... if it wasn't true that you didn't like me, why did you want me to think that you didn't?"

"I didn't."

"I thought you said...."

"Want *you* to think it. You're so innocent, John. Have we ever been alone together? Without Mary, I mean. Before now?"

"Not that I recall."

"So *who* do you think I wanted to think it?"

"Well, I can't remember who exactly was party to the proceedings on each and every occasion, other than Mary, of course.... Ahhhh, I see."

"Got there in the end."

"Well, um, thanks for, you know, putting the record straight. I appreciate it."

"Now that Mary isn't in the picture, you see."

"I see. Well, here we are alone together, then."

"And time for a slow one."

To make it fully clear that she was not referring to another whisky, Louise quickly drained her glass. Next, she put it down, in the decisive manner of one who has an appointment to keep. Then she stood and walked to the bed, whereupon she sat down again. Her air of perfect self-knowledge ruled out all possibility that the change of seating plan had been effected absent-mindedly.

John did not move.

"You're not in the least conflicted about this, are you?" she asked.

Love may be differently-abled vision-wise but this had no relevance in the present situation. Love, in anything more than its technical sense, was not the name of the game. To put it bluntly, there are some occasions when one really ought to look a gift horse in the mouth. Louise was not unattractive. She had kept well, or at least looked after herself well, and with respect to most skin-deep considerations (even her skin, which is so often a giveaway, especially around the neck) she met the general criteria of John's catholic tastes. He was not reluctant, therefore, nor even hesitant, with respect to the immediate present. It had to be that he was reluctant, or hesitant, only with respect to the medium-term hereafter.

"I don't want to get involved," he said, both to explain and to negotiate.

"I'm a married woman."

"Exactly."

"Don't worry about Howard."

"I'm not. I'm worried about you being a married woman."

"Point taken. But I like to keep the complications in my life simple."

As contractual undertakings go, that was clear enough. Yet John still did not move. It was only when he realised that if he hesitated any longer Louise might rescind the offer on the table, or rather on the bed, that he too stood and made his way over to her. Trying to understand the reason for his reluctance was not such a pressing matter, after all, and could reasonably be moved to the back-burner.

He sat down.

But then he got up again.

John was old-fashioned enough to think of himself as a New Man, at least in certain respects. For example, he was not in the least averse to bona-fide members of the fair sex taking a fair part of the lead, making fairly obvious advances and even being fairly explicit in their propositions. But whenever this egalitarian attitude had been put to the test in the past, he had been ready for it. Since all roads lead to Rome, he had felt able to take role-reversal in his stride, even to see it as a convenient shortcut. But Louise had jumped the gun. Masculine pride prevented him telling her that it's not just a matter of pressing buttons.

Louise took his hand and pulled him back into a sitting position.

"Relax," she counselled. "Breathe deeply. Concentrate on your breathing. Close your eyes and try to visualise your favourite landscape."

John did so. Just as he had fashioned a fairly accurate mental representation of Van Gogh's *Cornfield with Cypresses*, his central nervous system registered Louise's hand upon his thigh, at the aesthetically significant height at which a sculptor might balance a *Torso*. This is the very height, of course, at which one's experience of one's leg is not simply that of its useful extension, or status as a limb, something strictly optional, more that of its vital and necessary participation in the organic unity of the whole.

"Relax," Louise reminded him. "Lay down. Count backwards from fifty. Then say to yourself 'I am virile. I am virile. I am virile.'"

John had got to forty-four when he felt Louise's moist lips nudging his and her hand seeking some firmer purchase than hitherto. 'I am non-proactive, I am passive, I'm pathetic!' he said to himself. Getting at least one act together, he sat up.

"We could try *breathing together*," Louise suggested.

"Louise, go and sit in the armchair again."

"It's a bit narrow."

"Never mind. Just go and sit there."

She did so. John followed suit by returning to his upright wooden chair.

But you can't turn back the clock. And what a good thing that is! If you could, how many of us would be rewinding not just the odd few minutes here and there, but whole days, or weeks, or even years? Perfectionists might end up younger than their own children.

"Now I know what they mean by writer's block," Louise observed. "It's very *mental* work, isn't it?"

"I just need a bit more time."

"What unit of measurement are we using here?"

Louise, clearly, was a woman who knew what she wanted. But she was also, in the terms of her self-image, the soul of tact.

"Look," she added in a more supportive tone, "I honestly see nothing abject in your failure. I don't for a moment take that as representative of the best of your abilities. Take your time.... You'll be in tomorrow? About 7.30 again?"

John did not answer. A resigned expression, involving a slight sideways tilt of the head, was read by Louise as suggesting that all things are possible.

At the front door she turned back to him.

"Don't worry about it. That's the *worst* thing you can do. No, it isn't. The worst thing is to try to console or reassure yourself by.... Well, no man is an island, sufficient unto himself, is he? In my experience, *men* don't feel satisfied that way."

John tried to return to his writing. For the second time that day he found the supply-side economics of concentration in crisis.

The writing life. He really should try to fit in a daily workout.

THIRTEEN

"So you see, you can set your mind at rest," Louise assured Mary.

To be able to do so with both style and substance, she had opted for the ideal rather than the first available moment. To this end she had suggested an afternoon of spiritual retreat when all the minor cares of the workaday world would fade away and insight into self and soul could become, if not exactly on the cards, at least better than a long shot.

"Of course, I really couldn't see the point," she continued. "It's transparent to me that your fears are a symptom of your guilt feelings. You haven't been coping emotionally with having *both* your own car *and* your own lover. And even if – purely hypothetically – John were plotting the dire deed, he'd hardly name and shame himself at this early stage of the game. Even so, I sounded him out sufficiently to be able to say beyond a shadow of a doubt that, as closed books go, he wasn't trying to throw me off any scent or lead me up any garden path."

Louise politely closed the *Elle* on her lap, for it was Mary's turn to speak. She did, however, briefly glance back to the title of the article ("Feminist Fisti-Cuffs: Why Lace Is Empowering"), just to remind herself of what she had vaguely been half-reading.

"Well, thanks," came the response. "Thanks a million, in fact. I realise it must have been a trial for you, since you so obviously experience bad vibes in his presence. Are you *sure* he doesn't remember that pub?"

On this, she made eye contact, but appealingly, so as to rule out any suggestion of a missed métier in courtroom cross-examination. This was achieved via a large mirror.

"Absolutely," Louise reassured her bosom friend, leafing insouciantly through her glossy image-trove once again in order to underline her carefree sincerity. "I explored every avenue. By the way, don't show your age like that (I might even hear 'bad fibes' as in fibroids) – what I experience in his presence is called *negative energy*. Of course, I had to get him to loosen up a bit – for which I had to dig deep, by the way. It was very much a game of two halves. When I heard he was writing a novel, I told him, I realised I must have misjudged him and I'd really like to get more acquainted. I wouldn't be at all surprised if he thought that was just nudge-nudge, wink-wink, you know what men are like. He probably imagined my dislike for him was all an act I'd put on for your benefit and, now that you weren't in the picture, there I was openly advertising the hots I had for him. But I think I managed to negotiate that without undermining his masculinity."

"Well, thanks again. So you didn't come across anything in the way of dark and desperate thoughts? I mean, the reason he's writing a novel is... to write a novel?"

"I wouldn't go *that* far. It's not art for art's sake. But... look, Mary, I'm saying this entirely for your own good, even though it may hurt – I don't think John actually *loved* you, so *why* should he want to murder you?"

Mary failed to understand the logic of Louise's remark. She was not familiar with Oscar Wilde's *The Ballad of Reading Gaol*:

> Yet each man kills the thing he loves,
>   By each let this be heard,
> Some do it with a bitter look,

> Some with a flattering word.
> The coward does it with a kiss,
>   The brave man with a sword!

But even if she had been, she would probably not have empathised with the resigned austerity of tone. She might perhaps have found the languid pathos of Byron more congenial, in his *Don Juan*:

> Oh love, what is it in this world of ours
>   Which makes it fatal to be loved? Ah why
> With cypress branches hast thou wreathed thy bowers
>   And made thy best interpreter a sigh?
> As those who dote on odours pluck the flowers
>   And place them on their breast – but place to die;
> Thus the frail beings we would fondly cherish
> Are laid within our bosoms but to perish.

But she had not read this either. She did have a kind of instinctive feeling for crime passionnel – as of course we all do – but this did not stretch to malice aforethought. In any case, what had passion got to do with love? Love, as Mary conceived it, was the strange sense in which a couple could be somehow more than just two people.

Louise examined her hands, from various angles, while consulting the recommended skin-tone / varnish / digit-accessory schemes on page 189 (which ranged from 'The Mother of All Mitts' to 'Just The Hand Job').

"*In fact*," she added, "I found he had something of the strong, silent type. Even a touch of the dark horse. But, having said that, nothing to threaten you. I think he's happier living alone. Not in the happy-clappy sense, just less in the way of feeling a square peg in a round hole. I had a strong sense he was *on the point* of real get up and go – after I'd managed, you know, to break the ice. We got somewhere in the vicinity of a heart to heart, you see. Your fears – look, Mary, I'm saying this for your sake, even though you won't want to hear it – they're really a kind of *wish*. (Apart from expressing your guilt feelings, I mean.) You want to think that he's still thinking of you. But it's rather the diametric opposite."

Bzzzzzzzzzzzzzzzzzzzzzzz....

Mario strolled lightly over and removed the drier from Mary's hair. Dexterously he unfastened one roller, as a test.

"Perfection," he announced. "I shall now unveil my latest creation. I'm not just referring to your crowning glory, darling, I'm referring to *you*."

His fingers performed the task with an independence from each other but an overall sense of composition worthy of a concert pianist. His slim body, in its well fitting purple shirt and black trousers, curved and leaned this way and that like a confident sapling in a breeze which couldn't make up its mind which direction to blow from.

"After this, I shall no longer accept appointments. I shall only take commissions. But what were you girls talking about? It sounded so dreadfully seamy. Steamy I can take, but not seamy. I shall *not* lunch today. In fact I shall put up a sign: 'All reference to husbands – past, present or future – is forbidden in this salon.' This is a House of Pleasure, as only Woman, Lovely Woman, understands it (and a few of us boys, of course) – not a laundromat! Tell me, how on earth am I expected to make a New Woman of you if you come *attached*?"

The big moment had arrived. Mario took one big, springy step back and immediately raised his hands in – approximately – the gesture of someone held up at gun point. But the expression on his face was that of a child on Christmas morning, having just opened the present he had had every reason to expect.

"There! Mary, you are absolutely sumptuous, though I say so myself! Notice how the streak of honey suggests quite outrageously voluptuous indolence, while the wisp of red speaks volumes of your ability to take almost unimaginable initiatives! And the curls, the curls are Babylonian! But that is *you*, that is your contribution, darling – *I* had intended them to be Roman!"

But more services than one were offered in Mario's Tricho-Sculpture and Personal Identity Design Studio. With extravagant confidentiality, he bent to Mary's ear.

"Now I think I'm going to let you in on a little professional secret. If we really did believe that our ex wanted to murder us – ooh! what an ugly word ('ex' I mean) – we'd be having a bad hair day today, wouldn't we? But look at you!"

In point of fact Mary had pre-empted Mario's advice and was already fully engaged in the process of adjusting to her new self. Naturally she sought Louise's help in this.

"I wouldn't recognise you," said Louise.

So far so good. But what did it actually look like?

"Fantastic," said Louise.

In what precise sense?

"Great, great. But you *have* worn your hair the same way for the last fifteen years, so it takes a little getting used to."

But would they have to take a taxi?

Bzzzzzzzzzzzzzzzzzz....

Now it was Louise's turn to be unveiled.

"You do realise, don't you?" said Mario, "that I have *conceived* you – there's no other word for it – as a combination look. You must absolutely promise me from now on to go everywhere à deux."

Even so, the spotlight had shifted temporarily from Mary, giving her a little free time to try to exercise that higher form of intelligence, found only among a small part of God's (as distinct from Mario's) creation, including chimpanzees, dolphins and human beings, which involves the ability, nine times out of ten, to recognise oneself in a mirror.

Yes....

Yes... it was.

Yes... it was *her*!

FOURTEEN

Angela was at 21A, Bomber Harris Road, Clapham, ground floor, room 2, or, more informally, at John's place. She had just finished reading what she presumed a sufficient portion of his first four chapters and pronounced herself utterly underwhelmed. *Even* in Dickens, she pointed out, the body makes its presence conspicuous by its absence, in the deafening silence of its unmentionability. But in John's mode of writing, the body only made its *absence* felt by its absence!

"But it's not a detective novel," John excused himself. (For some reason, this made him feel he had to sit up on the bed.)

"I'm not talking about a *corpse*," Angela scoffed. "I'm talking about the bit which begins more or less under your nose!"

"You mean I ought to refer more to bodily functions?"

"Functions! The body, as I know it, doesn't have *functions*. It doesn't *have*, full stop. It *is*!"

"Is what?"

"*Desire!*"

"But I *know* that," said John, relieved to have found the right wavelength. "Look, it's there in black and white. Jonathan is passionately involved with Angelica, although he's still technically married to Marie. Because he desires her."

"I don't give a five second finger fest for *content*," Angela corrected him.

John sighed.

"Look," she explained, sensing the need to be more specific, "the problem lies in your first person

112

transcendent retrospection. Your *narrative I* is coming at us from the *other side*. Like a spirit. Disembodied. Dead. That implies either a happy ending or an unhappy ending. Right?"

John thought about this. When, at length, he felt that he had decoded the question, he was able to formulate what he believed to be a satisfactory answer.

"It implies something sufficiently worth looking back on."

"There you are then! Either way, desire appears as *satiable*. That's the problem."

John's own experience of desire was not such that the problem seemed quite so obvious. Whenever he had felt desire, he had felt it as some kind of need, more or less urgent, for satisfaction. Satisfaction, moreover, always seemed within the realms of possibility, if – all too often – only in principle.

He watched Angela stand, strangely distant, and go to the small, tiltable, rectangular mirror in its cheap pine frame which stood on the austere mantelpiece over the feeble gas fire. He watched her stare at her reflection, not as one who scrutinises imperfections or possible enhancements, but as one who is struggling to become more of an introvert. He knew he could look at her, for as long as she stood there, without her becoming aware of his eyes upon her.

He had the strange feeling that he had never really seen her before. She was of medium height, with a figure of the athletic type (the picture of health, that is, rather than pretty as a picture) which she displayed to advantage in well-fitting, low-waisted jeans and a low-cut shirt with girlie frills. Her upper body, thus, was subtly shifted towards the curvy end of the scale while, for balance, her lower limbs resisted any hint of languid voluptuousness by putting the emphasis on doing rather than being. In between (the meat in the sandwich, so to speak), the outfit gave an alluring glimpse of flesh, a perfect metonym of nakedness, precisely where the abdomen begins its gentle downward, inward curve.

Speak of the devil. The devil, desire, was in the details. John fancied he saw one stray, untrimmed, ascendant pubic hair, beckoning.

Not yet. For one thing there was the question of honour, for another there was the question of how.

"The point is, I don't yet know what the ending is," he said testily, to put business before – or perhaps in place of – pleasure.

"So *why* write *as if* you *do*?"

The simplicity of the words belied the utter obscurity of the question. John felt frustrated, now on a second count.

"Look, style-wise I'm after a clear window," he rallied. "Short, sharp sentences, let the verb do the work, no showy, superfluous or redundant adjectives, rigorously avoid adverbs (as one would the plague), with the passive voice being well and truly ruled out. Perhaps that gives the impression...."

"Oh my God, what a cliché! The true Orwellian nightmare. Everything Graham Greene learned from Enid Blyton," Angela intervened in a tone of restrained understatement. "My advice is, go for more in the way of ludic excess."

"For what?"

"Play-ful-ness," Angela spelt it out.

John had a distinct feeling of being hard done by. Rough justice, he felt, would have at least included Angela reading the entirety, and just deserts would have entailed some positive feedback to temper the negative. How often he had burnt the midnight oil and even (on some days) the candle at both ends! How often he had wrestled with variant syntactical constructions! How often he had clicked doggedly through the thickets of online thesauri! How sensitive he had become, a second nature, to the expressive possibilities of language – why, he was even now wondering if his thoughts would have been more convincingly thought with 'had he'.

A deal is a deal, John reminded himself. True, they had not shaken on it, nor was anything signed on any dotted line. But he was determined to stand up for his rights.

"Look, there's a section further on I'm quite proud of. It's the real McCoy. I mean, it's *me* – in the sense of authentic voice. Would you read it? And if you still want to damn it, please do so with faint praise. I seem to have shed my thick skin."

*   *   *

Angelica came straight from Cambridge to my bachelor pad to tell me she had got the job. I congratulated her.

Our love making was intense and wild, as it had been in the beginning, but for the first time I did not feel coaxed, guided, spurred on and reined in by turns, such that I had a vague post-coital recollection of having managed a clear round. Instead, Angelica seemed to want me to run wild, to offer herself to my unbridled lust. Her orgasms came thicker, faster, deeper, louder than ever before until, in the end, almost fainting, she appealed to me, appealed with fervent finger nails, with thrusting tongue, with levitating lower torso, to yield my seed unto her womb.

Naturally, I obliged.

"You know something?" she said, when she had sufficiently recovered a Newtonian sense of space and time. "That's the highest on the Richter scale I've ever come, not to mention the quantitative measure. How do you do it?"

"It takes two to tango," I replied.

She immediately understood what I was getting at. "Yes," she said. "You're right. This time, I didn't have my own agenda, did I?"

I said nothing. I was curious, of course, to know why she seemed so changed, why her tone had become stress free and why there was nothing of the computer animated kick boxer left in the way she held herself, when the doorbell rang.

I ignored it for as long as it took to get dressed. During this time, it rang twice more. Then, with some trepidation, I went to the front door. I was hoping it wouldn't be Marie's best friend, Lulu. When I had been living with Marie, Lulu had always made it abundantly clear that she thoroughly disliked me, but then Marie had always been around. Hence I was expecting a visit from her at any time, and not just to pop by. But, as I could hardly forget, Angelica was inside and possibly still in the state that nature intended.

Imagine my relief then to see Marie. She would never expect to be invited in.

"Surprise, surprise," she began.

"You can say that again," I responded.

"Aren't you going to invite me in?"

"No."

I seemed to have miscalculated. Marie was different in some way, more forthright, more assertive, more self-reliant, with more confidence in her feminine charms. The words of an old drinking companion, recently run into again, came back into my mind. "She'll have a fling or two or four, sow some wild oats, or whatever women can be said to do in that line, long overdue, get the backlog of promiscuity out of her system, and you never know, you may find her a damn sight better lay, altogether more finely tuned in all the relevant departments, than first time round." On the other hand, if she had found her way into a suitably liberating erotic entanglement, what was she doing here?

Having brusquely refused her suggestion, I felt the need to reinforce my position by sounding aggressive.

"What is it? An increase in the maintenance, I suppose."

"On the contrary. I don't want your money any more. I've found a job. I didn't come here to ask for anything, not even to express the hope that we can still be good friends. I *came to say thank you. You see, you helped me. You didn't intend to, but you helped me. You helped me find myself. By leaving me, you forced me to look within. I asked myself, what do I really want to be? A housewife? No, Jonathan. Not with you, not with anyone. So I've joined the editorial department of a major fiction publishing company. By the way, if you ever want to write a novel, here's my card."*

Angela stopped reading. Something, apparently, had occurred to her. She looked at John, an expression of intense cogitation lining her youthful face.

"So the *worm* that *turns* is *Marie*."

"Could be, I suppose," John replied. "I'm just letting my characters go where they would go, do what they would do, say what they would say."

Angela stood abruptly, throwing the printed A4 papers into the upper atmosphere of John's room. As a gesture, oddly, it did not ask to be interpreted as dismissive. It might have been celebratory.

"Could be! *Has* to be!!! It's the *swipe card*! Don't you see, 'worm' is such a *genderised* term! Think of *worm*, think of *man*! And what's the feminine form of worm? I'll tell you. Doormat! Doormats don't turn, they *get turned*! Yes, yes, *yes*! Marie *has* to be the worm!"

John had never been sure why he had chosen that title. He only knew that it was right, that it contained some deep truth that would reveal itself in time. Writing was a journey of discovery. He did not feel that journey was over.

"I don't know," he prevaricated. "OK, so Marie now has a job. In effect she's left Jonathan behind her. But the story is told from his point of view. How will Marie come back into it? There's no way I'll make Jonathan start writing a novel. A novel with a central character who writes a novel, I mean, how many times has *that* been done! True, the whole thing is autobiographical, of course, but only *in essence*, not in every detail."

Angela sat down again. She looked at him with an expression of intense surprise lining her youthful face.

"It's... autobiographical?"

"Yes. Autobiographically based, anyway. Jonathan – John. Marie – Mary. Angelica – well, you."

"But... but... that puts everything in a different light. Look, John, I'm going to have to think through what an autobiographically based post-modernist novel might be like. If it isn't a bigger and better microchip, even."

"Sorry?"

"What in EDL was called a contradiction in terms."

"EDL?"

"English as a Dead Language."

She fell silent. Perhaps, in part, she was struggling to come to terms with why she had overlooked what now seemed glaringly obvious. But probably not. Her province, after all, had been 'form,' not content.

John had retrieved almost all his sheets of paper when Angela stood up again and confronted him.

"Jonathan *doesn't* have a daughter!"

"Don't jump to conclusions. Maybe he does. Maybe he just hasn't mentioned her."

The expression lining Angela's youthful face was now one of intense incipient intermittent explosive disorder. "I'm leaving!" she shouted, knocking the autobiographically based manuscript out of his hands.

"Why?"

"You're a complete, utter and absolute bastard!"

"Why?"

"*Why? Why?* Don't you realise that I can only work with a protagonist whose parenting skills I can *respect*? Don't you realise that if I let myself *get into* your first person narration, I'll have to face the fact that Jonathan is just like my *real father*? Don't you realise that that might even be what I *really want*? Don't you realise that if I let myself get *that* involved, even professionally, in your autobiography... **ALL RIGHT!!!,** your autobiographically *based*, fictional elaboration of what it's *like* to be a bastard – I'd only start waiting for you to *write me out of your life too*? Don't you realise that the resulting panic attacks would cause me to *fail in my career*? At **OXFORD!!!**"

In an emotional sense, John had battened down the hatches and was trying to weather the storm. But he didn't have a duck's back and something in the rain of recrimination got through to him. The only option left was to put a brave face on it, but the heroic code felt more than usually alien to him. From where he was standing, the expression on his face felt more sheepish than valiant.

Angela stood still for a moment and looked straight at him. 'Why?' her look seemed to ask. 'Why what?' John tried to look back. Without the slightest corporeal linguistic hint of 'I asked first', she then walked out – decisively without storming and casually without breezing. This, coupled with the way she did not condescend to slam the door, seemed to imply that – as walks go – here was one not just out of his room.

It was out of his life.

FIFTEEN

It is better to have loved and lost than never to have loved at all. On the other hand, losing a loved one is a crushing blow – especially when the lost loved one remains alive and kicking. There's no point moaning about the slings and arrows – let alone the microaggressions – of outrageous fortune. Desertion is deliberate. It takes the wind out of the sails of one's ego as well as the joie out of vivre.

John had not heard from Angela for the past three days. Sub specie aeternitatis, three days are a drop in the ocean – but they can still feel like an age. His creativity had not been blocked as a result; it had just failed to put all its eggs in one basket, thereby causing him to fall between two stools. He had pressed on with his novel but in stop-start mode, spending too long mulling over the exact wording of the dozen or so text messages he had sent Angela, all of which had gone unanswered. Chaff in the wind.

Still, hope springs eternal in the human breast. Hope is adaptable, even more than children are. It has fall-back positions.

There are plenty more fish in the sea, for example.

For John, however, that item of folk wisdom was not the panacea it would once have been. True, on Louise's second visit he had been less unrelaxed. And on her third, earlier that same day, he had felt reasonably confident that she had felt the earth shift a little, although he couldn't put it past a Life Skills Therapist to fake that kind of positive feedback. Louise, he was discovering, had panache between the sheets. An out of body experience (one of those attained in and through the body) may have been looming large. The problem was that his private life was no longer something merely between him and his conscience. It had been upgraded to a source of inspiration. It was now the well-spring of his imagination. An amour strictly on the side was out of the question. For John had moved beyond the relatively straightforward life-goal of having his cake and eating it. Now he ate his cake to regurgitate it. But not to chew the cud. To reengineer, restructure or... re-recipe it.

Then it struck him – cake is cake, even if it has no icing on it. If he was obliged to forget Angela (in the curious sense of consigning her to memory), then he would simply co-consign Angelica to a Part One. Any heart-wrenching this involved would add a dimension. You can't make an omelette without breaking eggs.

'I have to admit, when I set out on this path I didn't think of it as a long and lonely road,' he reflected. 'Long, yes. But the novel has taken on a life of its own even if the collaboration has died the death. The man in me may be gutted but the author is the stronger for it. This is no time to cut and run. The only exit strategy is to stay the course.'

And so John made a virtue of necessity....

*   *   *

The world is made up of two kinds of people – those who don't like someone walking just behind them in the street and those who don't like someone walking just in front of them. I was in the latter camp. So was Angelica, did she but know it. We were two of a kind, kindred spirits, made for walking side by side down the long road of life, but she was being held back by something she hadn't been able to take in her stride.

Her father had died when she was at the worst possible age – thirteen.

I suspected she saw me as a father figure, although the lived-experience-gap was only fifteen years. At first this flattered me. I must have looked stronger, wiser, more stable and less fallible in her innocent eyes than in the morning mirror. For a time I indulged it – she seemed so vulnerable. But it began to have a strange effect on me, especially when it started filtering through to what little spare consciousness I had while we were making love.

In the end, I found myself wondering what she was thinking.

Angelica had no idea of this, for it didn't undermine my masculinity. Then I noticed how she kept her eyes closed from start to finish. I'd noticed this before, from day one, in fact, but I'd put it down to ecstasy. Now I began to wonder. From my point of view, I was making love to her. But what about from her point of view?

From my point of view, my point of view was of more immediate significance. But it wasn't the be all and end all. Sex, to me, was communication.

I knew Freud, of course, if only as an integral part of our cultural heritage. I knew the nuclear family had a subtext. It wasn't pretty, but I didn't feel like sweeping it under the carpet. I liked my carpets clean on both sides. So I toyed with the idea of asking her to look at me, at some immediately pre-orgasmic moment. The precise timing would be tricky. I had to catch her with her guard down but while she was still centred ('grounded' would be asking too much).

My chance came one evening in late December. Or so I thought. The night was dark and stormy. The wind roared in the chimney of my fireplace like a caged wild beast. It was the kind of night to make you think seriously of those in peril on the sea, the kind of night, in other words, for truly wild communication – as long as you were indoors. I lit a fire, dimmed the lights and watched the writhing bodies of the flames dance. It looked one hell of a party.

Spiritually, I wasn't convinced by Pascal's wager. In fact I reasoned that if we only had this life, the best bet was to make the most of it. Even so, I was open-minded. I hadn't ruled out the leap of faith, though I wasn't planning on it. But where revelation was concerned, my verdict was an unequivocal 'not proven'.

That's no non sequitur.

"I need to talk," said Angelica, on arrival, in fact on the doorstep. So there really were more things in heaven and earth than had been dreamed of in my philosophy. Telepathy, to say the least. Don't ask me how, but I just knew what she wanted to talk about. The only difference was, I had wanted to investigate the issue in flagrante, not before.

But I didn't negotiate that point. She'd expressed a need, not a want. I could have used the same terminology, but she had seized the time. We went inside.

"Go ahead."

"Well, you know how my father died when I was thirteen?"

"No. I know he died, and when, but not how."

"I meant 'that'. Not how."

Angelica was always so on the ball linguistically. This wasn't like her.

"How did he die, in fact?"

"Suicide. But that's irrelevant, Jonathan."

The poor kid. "Is it?" I said pointedly.

"Yes. Death is such an existential fact that the cause has nothing to do with it. The point is, one day he was there, the next day he wasn't. That had knock-on effects. To be specific, I couldn't accept it. Do you realise what that means? It means I'm still thirteen."

"Psychologically?"

"Emotionally. I'd hardly be teaching at Cambridge if I were thirteen cognitively, would I?"

She seemed back to her normal self. At least, I was back to my normal feeling of having said the wrong thing. Sometimes I missed the kind of woman who would only take umbrage at remarks like "You're looking tired".

"Anyway," she went on, "yesterday I suddenly realised something. It had been staring me in the face all along, but I must have been keeping my eyes closed. You see... you see... he was thirty-nine when he died! The same age as you!"

I didn't need long to grasp the point. But I needed a few moments to think of an appropriate response.

"So?"

"So this is... goodbye."

"Why?"

"Because you're not my father."

From where I was standing, that seemed a definite plus. But I knew what she meant. A healthy dose of realism is all very well, but the resulting non-viability of her fantasy made her suddenly unbearably alone. She felt that now she had to face that existential fact. That's tough at thirteen, I thought. She needed affection.

I went to put my arm around her. She didn't object, didn't resist, in fact didn't seem to notice. I was now sitting on the arm of my old leather armchair, in which she seemed so petite and lost. There was room for two. I slid down beside her. My arm moved down from her shoulder to her waist, increasing its pressure gently but noticeably.

She broke free and stood up.

"You want me to sit on your lap?"

"I'm just giving you affection."

She looked bemused. "What's that?"

My heart bled for her. Her mother must have clammed up on widowhood and her previous boyfriends must have had the emotional intelligence of boys. I thought of trying to explain, but that's like trying to tell someone what an orange tastes like when they've never tried one. It's better to reach for the fruit bowl.

"It's this."

I stood, took her in my arms and stroked her hair with my right hand. My left hand made base camp between her shoulder blades, whence I moved it up and down, carefully reducing its claim upon her as it reached the small of her back. This way contact between us remained focused in the upper thoracic region. My right fingers then suggested that her head rest upon my shoulder. Of course, I made sure her face was turned away from me. Only if she started to sob would I turn her head inwards. I then kissed the back of her head, keeping my lips closed, their weight light and the duration limited.

I felt her arms circle my waist. I felt her elbows grip as her palms pressed imploringly against my back. She wanted more affection, obviously. No wonder, since she seemed never to have experienced it before.

Then her knee rubbed mine. This might have been a nervous twitch, brought on by the release of so much emotion, but I didn't think so. The movement was both too slow and too extended. I knew that knees were out of bounds for affection, at least in England, but how could she be expected to know that?

And I liked it.

I was just musing that our love making might have been even more intense and wild than it had been at the beginning – and once since – if I had been prepared to take advantage of a tragic childhood, when the doorbell rang.

Angelica disengaged from my embrace. She seemed to be working on the assumption that I was going to answer it. What could I do in the circumstances? I stood and looked deep into her eyes. The idea was to give her a couple more moments to say, "Ignore it".

"Someone's at the door," she pointed out instead.

SIXTEEN

The common lot of mortal man is to grow old. Today, with improved nutrition, living conditions and healthcare, growing old is not what it used to be – nasty, brutish, short, and kicking in at a relatively young age; on the contrary, it offers new opportunities. But we still don't go out in a blaze of glory. Time goes by, as always, insisting on its arrow by working away at its ravages. In the final analysis, cosmetic surgery is no match for the increasing entropy of this mortal coil.

Enough hard science. You're as old as you feel.

I hadn't really felt older than Angelica. I hadn't been trying to recapture my youth. I'd never lost it.

It was strange therefore, not to say ironic, that I suddenly started feeling my age as I made my way to the front door. In fact, I was experiencing it to the full. But why? Then it clicked. If I was as young as I felt, so was she – and I'd just found a thirteen year-old's knee very seductive. It wasn't automatic entry to the sex offenders' register, but it made me feel that combining father-figurehood with pleasure was a tricky business.

I was in too deep.

Yes, the ring of the doorbell had been a blessing in disguise. I opened more willingly than I had launched out in that direction.

I have never seen such an extraordinarily ordinary person as the man who stood at my portal. Everything about him was ordinary. His physique was perfectly average. His posture was upright but lacked ambition. His face was strikingly nondescript. His expression was disconcertingly neither this nor that. His shoes were sound, recently polished but far short of shiny. His raincoat had seen better days but was still serviceable. His hat was not at any angle. His voice was just doing its job.

I took an instant dislike to him. Don't get me wrong – some of my best friends are ordinary. But they also have redeeming features. One has a raucous laugh, for example; another has amusingly simian ears. But this individual was bereft of all distinction. Individual, in fact, wasn't the word. It was almost uncanny. He was a photo-fit of homo sapiens, deduced by aliens from a sequenced genome.

He said what had brought him thither. But he wouldn't take No for an answer.

"Look," I insisted. "On the evidence before me, I really don't want to be saved."

But I had been! The next step was to go back in and get rid of Angelica.

"God's judgment is nigh, you know. In the best-case scenario, you'll be cast into outer darkness. There's no peace for the wicked there either. But seek and ye shall find. Try reading this. It comes at no cost."

"If I promise to read it, will you move on?"

"Same time tomorrow then? Around 7.30?"

I perused the colourful but puritanically matt cover of the pamphlet he had given me as I made my way back inside. The four photo-realistic beaming faces suggested not so much the joy of having discovered Our Lord as that of belonging to a perfect nuclear family. Was there such a thing, I wondered? Did it really exist?

This train of thought was a mistake. I should have been thinking of the right form of words. When it came to the crunch, I was tongue-tied – like an adolescent on his first date.

"Angelica?"

"Yes."

"I..."

"Yes."

"Where were we?"

She came over, put her arms around me, pressed herself imploringly against more than a modicum of my torso, and began that heavenly, divine, slow, extended, rhythmic motion of her knee. For a moment it was as though there had been no doorbell, no extraordinarily ordinary individual, no glimpse of the true path, but I was still clutching 'Ten Ways to Avoid Perdition' in my hand. I looked over her shoulder at the family basking innocently in its subtextlessness. I was torn. At best I was falling between two stools. I had to decide!

Angelica broke away.

"What are you reading?" she asked.

I showed her. She laughed.

"I'd never had thought it," she mocked. "I'm off."

"Angelica, wait! I took it just to get rid of him."

"That's what they all say. You seem to have found it gripping enough. Goodbye!"

"Goodbye? As in see you? Au revoir? Parting is such sweet sorrow, even?"

"No. As in fuck off, you superannuated tosspot!"

"As in... it's been nice knowing you? Fun while it lasted?"

"Look, excuse the Latin bit. Let's back up, shall we?"

"OK."

"OK. Goodbye."

"As in no regrets, perhaps?"

"Goodbye."

"As in let's just put it down to experience, then?"

"Goodbye."

"Or more a case of if you could just have your time over again?"

"Jonathan..."

"I'm just trying to catch the nuance."

"Jonathan, there is no nuance."

"I see. As bad as that."

"I feel free."

"Would you mind if we backed up again?"

"Where to?"

"How about the first goodbye."

"OK. Goodbye."

I paused for a moment. I looked into her eyes. I gave a small but sincere smile, principally by means of my eyes. "Goodbye," I said in a polite, restrained tone, with an underlying note of deep appreciation, stoical acceptance and profoundly unexpressed misery.

Angelica laughed. "Trevor Howard! That's Trevor Howard in Brief Encounter! *Adultery à l'anglaise! Christ, anyone'd think we never* actually *fucked!"*

SEVENTEEN

I don't keep a diary but I do know that the human animal continues to live life on a day to day basis. Why else do so many of us fail to arrange a comfortable pension in time or to give up smoking before it's too late to complete the London Marathon, even in a wheelchair? The night, even a bad one, takes us out of time, out of the familiar world, out of existence, as much when we choose to while away the small hours watching a late film as when safely in the land of Nod. Every morning is a new beginning, a time to put one's best foot forward, another chance, a window of opportunity. If we were the rational creatures of mythology, we would wake up, or at least get up, consciously closer to our death. Instead, we rise unconsciously closer to our birth. Only in the evenings do we feel another day older. Of course, there are exceptions. Some, such as the clinically depressed, find getting out of bed a serious challenge. But they are the exceptions which prove the rule, by needing treatment.

The next morning, in other words, all was right with the world. At least, I felt relieved. Free. Ready to give life my best shot. A weight had been taken from my mind.

Why do relationships of the kind that make three a crowd have to be so complicated, I asked myself? Why is bonding pure and simple, as and when required, about as difficult to come across in this life as the philosopher's stone? Why is emotional give and take invariably something no trained accountant could make head or tail of? Why is it that among a woman's manifold needs is one to keep moving the goalposts and another never to understand that that's what's she's doing? Why....

But that was beating my head against a brick wall. I'd go to the pub, strike up a conversation, down a pint or two and engage in some constructive geo-political thinking instead. That's easier than trying to fathom the opposite sex – and less of a waste of time.

"You don't hear the phrase 'free world' much these days," I observed to Leonard. He had been already ensconced in The Sword and Ploughshare and I therefore naturally did the first honour. With pints in hand, we felt free to set the world to rights. "For a while we had a good go at replacing it with 'civilisation'. But in my book that entails a contradiction. How can you have civilisation versus evil and a clash of civilisations at one and the same time? No, no, I suggest we revert to 'free world,' but redefining what we mean by 'free' as not just free to fail in a small business, but free to think for ourselves or at the very least to choose who does our thinking for us."

"Nice idea in principle," Leonard responded. "The snag is that nobody thinks ideology post German reunification."

"You're missing the point. 'Free' in my sense rules out Islam."

"That's as may be, but somehow the 'theocratic menace' doesn't trip off the tongue like the 'red menace' used to. What about that, eh?"

"True enough. The nitty-gritty is, however, that civilization, as the contemporary term for us as against them, doesn't have a suitable opposite, not even implicitly. 'Evil' may have served the turn on the other side of the pond, post twin towers, but here a more nuanced approach has always been necessary, one consistent with there having actually been a Renaissance. Barbarism is technically accurate, of course, but for some reason it seems about two thousand years out of date, more's the pity, except in the case of a certain class of football fans. And as for savagery, it contradicts every accepted tenet of PC and really ought to be the s-word."

"Agreed there's a nut to crack here. But it's not civilisation as such. It's western civilisation. What precisely is it? Tell me that, if you can. Do we have any idea what we're fighting for in this war? You only have to scratch below the surface to see that liberal values are less well defined than the Holy Trinity. I sometimes ask myself, has the Enlightenment project run out of steam? Might it even be withering on the branch? We still have the language of Shakespeare, of course – we as on this sceptered isle, that is. Stateside too, let us accept that fact. But how many of us fully appreciate the burgeoning threat posed by English as a Foreign Language? Think of the vast hordes for whom words like 'sceptered' will never trip off the tongue, both outside and, increasingly, inside this fair realm. English could very well go the way of Latin, you know. Sic transit gloria mundi, of course, but then what becomes of the Special Relationship? In any case, our transatlantic cousins have their own demographic problem, hushed up though it is. Sensitivity awareness guidelines prevent their even admitting it, you see, let alone subjecting it to free democratic debate (they really should take a lesson from Israel). Do you have any idea by how much the Hispanic outperforms the Anglo-Saxon on the birthrate indicator? How on earth will a wall stop that, eh? Yes, there's a re-run of 1588 on the horizon, no doubt about it. Odd, isn't it? Plus ça change, plus c'est la même chose, as the Irish say. But back in the days of Good Queen Bess, the enemy wasn't invisible and wasn't everywhere. There was the odd terrorist, of course, Guy Fawkes for example. But what's gunpowder compared, say, to Sarin or smallpox?"

It was exactly the kind of conversation I needed.

"True enough, but more likely these days it'll be a heavy goods vehicle. Easier to get hold of."

"Quite. How is the old sex-life?" Leonard interrupted, breaking every unwritten rule in the book.

"I'd rather not talk about that."

"That bad?"

"No, no. I mean I came here with the express intention of talking about something else."

"Hors de combat, eh? Time to hitch back up with the duchess, by the sound of it. A man has to do what a man has to do, for which a bird in the hand is vastly to be preferred. And the bottom line is, even a significant other fits that bill, faute de mieux. You never know, you may find Marie a damn sight better lay, altogether more finely tuned in all the relevant departments, than first time round. She'll have got the backlog of promiscuity – well, logjam's a better word in Marie's case (speaking as an observer, you understand) – out of her system by now, you see."

I should have realised Leonard was prone to raise such a subject, but my need for masculine fellowship, with its no frills, outward looking, hands on and solution-oriented approach to the world had made me overlook the fact that by profession he was a psychoanalyst.

"You've said that before."

"A fling or two will have loosened her up, greased the right parts, in other words."

"Look, Leonard, I did not leave Marie so that she could get more in touch with her libido, and even if I had done, it would not have been so that a little later I could live out the Oedipal fantasy of climbing into bed with a sexually experienced, sexually active mother figure."

"That's what they all say."

In spite of the fact that nature really was calling, I felt as if I was beating a retreat to the gents, and that without so much as a parting shot. But I couldn't have been running away from my thoughts. They came with me.

I'd been married to Marie, so I knew her. She had never played the field. She might have let her hair down behind my back, but not to go the whole hog. A little flirtation was all the spice of life she wanted. She read magazines like Health & Fitness, so I had realised early on that ours was not to be an open marriage. She had never given me the impression that she was inclined to think of sex as a hundred and ten percent physical experience. Hence when I first broke the monogamy seal (it took a few years), I had spared her the details. All of them. She was naïve, trusting and, as far as I could tell, believed in fairy tales. Who was I to undermine her 'ever after'?

It had never occurred to me that my departure might be a precondition of her getting more in touch with the animal in her. Either this was because I really did know her, in a sense that could be projected into her future, or because I didn't care.

"In fact, Leonard," I said, on returning to our table, "I'm not the least bit curious whether Marie's lower nature has now moved up a gear or even onto a higher plane of existence. If I were ever to go back to her, it would be to take an active interest in the roses and the wallpaper, something of that ilk. She'd see to that. Now, to get back to weightier matters. In my humble opinion, the way to put the Great back into Britain is not to do another Henry VIII, unshackling ourselves from Brussels as he did from Rome, but simply to drop the Britain. I propose a name change, or rebranding. How about Great Englishland? The analogy is with Deutschland, you see, thus killing two birds with one stone. First, it downsizes the French connection (which is so passé), but more to the point, it emphasizes the language – wherein our greatness truly lies. I don't share your view of EFL as a threat. Think of the leverage in having the lion's share of the global means of expression market...."

EIGHTEEN

Lulu had come round to my bachelor pad, as I had long anticipated, to put the record straight.

"It's really not necessary," I said. "You see, I know why you always made it so obvious you disliked me. Marie was always around, wasn't she?"

"I didn't know men could be so tuned in."

"My motto is, 'Never make a marine molehill out of the tip of an iceberg'. But thanks, anyway."

"She's not only not around right now, she's not even in the picture.... I'm sure you can read between my lines."

"Affirmative, but on one condition. I don't want to get involved."

"I'm a married woman."

"Exactly."

"Don't worry about Hugh."

"I'm not. I'm worried about you being a married woman."

"I get the message. But I wouldn't dream of digging my claws in - apart from during orgasms. You see, I unreservedly anticipate you going back to Marie."

Twice in one day. It was becoming monotonous.... Or was it?

"Working hard is he, Hugh?

"-aholically. I hardly know what to do with myself. All afternoon."

Message received. I waved the bottle of scotch in her direction.

"I don't mind if I do."

We raised glasses. "Here's to..." I began.

"Keeping the complications in one's life simple."

"I'll drink to that."

She downed the scotch, kicked off one shoe, then the other. Then she turned her back to me, to draw my attention to a zip fastener which extended all the way from the nape to the sacrum. She seemed to take a helping hand with disrobing for granted, as an unquestionable feature of social order, like an aristocrat before the French Revolution. But it didn't make me feel like a lady in waiting.

Our love making was intense and wild, but I didn't put that down to the novelty value. The way I approached it, it had simply been in the pipeline, one of those obligations to oneself – for both of us – like a dental check up, something that can be put off, but which has to happen sometime. I mean I was travelling light, emotionally. Free as a bird – or rather, uninhibited as a budgie in the wild.

I did Lulu's zip up. As an act of closure, there wasn't only a dress involved. If you want to be able to look back on life, I reflected, you first have to live it. And I just had.

Then, for some unaccountable reason, I thought of Oscar Wilde. He was wrong about truth, I felt. He was right that it's rarely pure, but not that it's never simple.

Why, that very morning I had been torturing myself with unanswerable questions, which all, in the last analysis, boiled down to this: what exactly makes a woman tick? I'm not talking about pressing buttons. I learnt long ago that there's no X that marks the G-spot. If there is such a location, it has the gypsy in its soul; in other words, it wanders. I'm referring to how two mature adults of complementary biology can arrive at mutual understanding.

Then I had one of those mind-expanding (as against boggling or blowing) revelations which come in a flash or not at all.

You don't reach a profound insight by thinking things through. That's flogging a dead horse with respect to knowing what it's all about. But if you have eyes to see and ears to hear, and provided you keep your finger on the pulse, you realise that life sends all the right signals. Even so, that's not enough. The right signals have to add up – to a whole that's greater than the sum of its parts. You can't make this happen. The readiness is all.

And describing an insight is much like explaining a joke.

But here goes, anyway.

If I say we must cut our coats according to our cloth, it will sound like I'm advocating a mere reality check and kissing wishful thinking a sad goodbye. No, for me that phrase suddenly resounded with no note of resignation.

But you've also got to know yourself – that is, your own size.

Then what if you don't have enough cloth to fit? But that's just a rational objection. It's wide of the mark and, ipso facto, off-message. Such a mechanistic approach can't get beyond 'solutions' like downsizing or taking an early bath. No, there's enough cloth by definition! Why had Lulu's and my love making been such a resounding success? Because I hadn't expected anything more than that!

And why was that? It was simple, so simple. Lulu was a mature woman. She knew what she wanted. That left me free to be an equal partner in a relationship between two of a kind. Not the kind of two of a kind I had felt in the case of Angelica. Angelica had a knack of introducing fuzzy logic into every facet of binarity, let alone coupledom. She'd made me feel that not only did I have a need to meet her needs, but also to find out on her behalf exactly what they were! Poor Angelica. She was mixed up. I'd found that touching until I'd realised it was catching.

Objectively, I didn't blame her. Mature self-awareness isn't easy these days, not even at a ripe old age. I blame the social media, imbibed like mother's milk, unthinkingly, by one of her tender years. Our sweetest dreams, our worst nightmares, are all pre-programmed – and short on both the agony and the ecstasy. People shop till they drop, literally, looking for the image that fits, their passport to the multiplex scenarios on offer. All photoshopped. It's the social media that peddle the shifting sands of illusion, a phantasmagoria of style over substance in which modern man is content to deposit his head.

But if you're in true self-search mode, you'd better expect the unexpected. In my case, what I wouldn't have guessed in a month of Sundays was not that youth is wasted on the young, but that there were two ways of looking at that fact; as a glass, it was either half-empty or half-full. In that sense, my happiness was my call.

Yes, it's liberating to realise that it's sufficient to look on the bright side. Full scale denial may seem the soft option, but it's shooting yourself in the foot. Denial throws the baby out with the bath water. It's a kind of party pooping, by the back door.

Life's too short to take the rough edges off, but they don't have to add up to a catalogue of disasters. And you'd literally have to move heaven and earth to make the sun stand still. Given the energy deficit involved, that'd be like sitting up to see in the end of the world. A Herculean effort down the drain.

No, let's get back to nature instead. Sexing up sex is dumbing down desire. Unforgettable moments don't come in individual wrappers. You can't have a field day gilding lilies. Or if that's asking too much, let's at least get back to the art of being artless.

The quality of life isn't set by pacesetters. A pacemaker is just a life-support machine. But think of the dinosaurs. We have overweening arrogance but they had overreaching size. What's the difference? Nemesis doesn't take prisoners.

It's hard to touch base with a vegetable and you can't be a rank and file member of the old boy's club. In the case of advanced years the only remedy is worse than the disease. But the journey is more important than the destination. Adhocracy rules. Making the most of much of a muchness is better than counting on manna from heaven.

And how little the cult of youth understands! How angst-ridden the overgrown juvenile in the street's concern with batting averages! They are blinded by the leaps and *bounds of technology, digitalise all lived experience, live not life but life styles, yearn not for oneness with themselves but to be part of some scene, in an in crowd and where it's at. And all for what?*

To put off the moment of truth. To avoid looking in the mirror.

But that's a blind alley. Worse, it's digging a hole for yourself. I would throw a birthday party instead. Since the ripeness is all, all I had to do was embrace the opportunities implicit in grasping the nettle. I had no regrets about how I'd graced the game of youth – no, no regrets – but that was what it was, a game. The real thing begins at forty.

Of course, all these thoughts took less real time than it did for Lulu to get shod.

"And I 'unreservedly anticipate' there's more where that came from," she said appreciatively.

"My only limited resources," I agreed, "are financial. Yes. So I'm thinking of giving this place up."

*   *   *

John paused. He felt uneasy.

He had been in full stride and top gear. Why had he paused? Why did he feel uneasy?

'Of course,' he realised. 'Jonathan does *not* have limited resources. He lives in an elegant, spacious, ground floor apartment furnished with taste.'

His eye took in his own domestic circumstances.

Outside, it was the first sunny day for over three weeks. In fact there was wall to wall sunshine. True, the walls were on the low side – it was January.

But inside you wouldn't have known it. The narrowness of the street, the ancient deposits of dirt on the window, the grey-brown net curtain, all conspired in shedding gloom. Not just that. Gloom and doom.

And that bed. There was only a wrong side to get out of.

A previous occupant had carved his initials on the small, dilapidated table that served as a desk.

F. O.

Probably Irish.

Where are the snows of yesteryear? Where are yesterday's men?

Yes, there was only one thing for it – a rationalisation of the status quo with respect to complications. The time had come to consider his position.

PART THREE

Back to the drawing board

NINETEEN

John had suggested a meeting on neutral ground but Mary preferred to play at home. In a wine bar – or even worse, in a pub – he'd be every inch the gentleman, gallant, courteous and in control. But paying for their drinks wouldn't balance *any* books! No, *she* would call the tune. She would even invite him to make himself at home – a magnanimous gesture that ought sufficiently to rub his nose in it.

The planning stage, for Mary, was a pleasure in itself. She ran over various selections from the book that she would throw at him, in each of which she found a new home truth with which to twist the knife. She realised of course that when push came to shove it might not be all one way; John might have an ace up his sleeve which she hadn't foreseen. But she held the high ground and had recently googled enough power words to rub that fact well in. The pound of flesh was in the bag – although that was not quite the price she would put on his return to the fold. Her central demand, which would remain implicit, was that his tail remain between his legs for considerably more than a cooling off period. But she had other, more substantive claims too.

Was she counting her chickens before they were hatched? No. John had not said why he wanted a meeting. But that said it all.

And Ron was no longer a factor in the equation. On their ninth date, he had failed to materialise. Immediately Mary saw the writing on the wall. This was confirmed shortly after by phone.

All things pass away, including the good things in life. But good things, rightly viewed, also leave something good behind them, such as a warm glow. Think of a balmy summer's day followed by a glorious sunset. And since the sunset is itself a good thing, it too, rightly viewed, leaves something good behind it, such as hundreds of likes for the photo you posted. This feature, after all, is what makes good things good.

At the end of her whirlwind romance (or rather, at the end of the process of coming to terms with its end, which had taken a full further twenty-four hours), Mary felt herself refreshed, as by a gentle breeze. Another in her situation might have felt granted a new lease of life or even reborn as a woman, but Mary was not given to hyperbole. It had done her a power of good. She had discovered her true touchy-feely self. It had been just what the doctor ordered (the kind of doctor who saw the whole person and didn't hand out pills as if they were Smarties). She had recorded all the landmark events in her diary, in order that the memory should not pale into insignificance, but laconically by writing "Yes" (on three occasions with an exclamation mark – "Yes!" – and once repetitively (but not redundantly) – "Yes! Yes!"), where a seventeen or eighteen year-old might have drawn a little heart. In other words she had lived the experience while maturely remaining her age, by discovering the joy of sex for its own sake.

And fortunately Ron had refused her suggestion that they remain good friends, by pointing out that they could hardly remain what they had never been. The remark had hurt at the time, since Mary still had some tendency to confuse categories, but she had quickly come to realise that looking back on carnal knowledge of an almost complete stranger had more in the way of warm glow and less in the way of rose-tinted spectacles. She even regretted having solicited his name.

If truth be told, a significant part of that feeling of refreshment lay in the absence of qualms of conscience. Her new amoral self surprised her. She did not need to tell herself that she had got involved on the rebound, nor even that she had not made any of the first moves. Instead she felt confident that if (a) John had after all left her for another woman, (b) his affair had now gone the way of all flesh-related things, and (c) he now felt the need to get it off his chest, her lips would remain sealed concerning Ron.

Only one thing troubled her: if John *had* been less than honest with her, why hadn't she known? There had been no smoking gun, of course, but a woman is supposed to know. A woman should know in the complete and utter absence of the kind of evidence that stands up in court. Not just the tiniest but the most ambiguous of tell-tale signs should be more than enough.

The worst-case scenario here was not just that she hadn't known, but that she was about to be the last one to find out. A second, more philosophical problem was that when a woman just knows, she presumably does so because she knows her husband. Hence....

Then it occurred to Mary. *If* no other woman was involved, *then* she might feel guilty about Ron. From this it followed (logically enough) that almost certainly she'd got involved with Ron because she *had* known. It was just that she hadn't known she had known.

This solution seemed to accord perfectly with the way a woman is supposed to know. Mary had simply needed to get more in touch with her intuition. Now that she had done so, she began to explore its limits. Certainly the other woman *had* been a younger woman. But how young? Intuition isn't exact about things like numbers, but it answered the question anyway: John had certainly been making a fool of himself. And certainly she, the junior partner, had broken it off. Not John. But how young? In fact, was "woman" the right word? This was not just a semantic question. She, Mary, could cope with the green-eyed monster, but not with a total loss of respect for her husband.

At this moment Jennifer came back from school. Moodily, she went straight to her room.

Mary had lately become aware of a tension in her relationship with her daughter. She assumed that a child's natural tendency to blame the deserted parent was the root cause. It was not. How could Mary have known that Jennifer was experiencing what it really meant to be a female of the species and needed nothing other than to be alone – miserably, longingly, exquisitely alone, with only Mr Winsom in her thoughts.

(Mr Winsom was Ms Pringle's temporary replacement, the latter having recently given birth to a bouncing baby boy.)

Even so, there was a modicum of truth in Mary's diagnosis, for on this particular day Jennifer was missing her father. The reason was as follows. Her best friend Georgina had found out what an 'orientation' was. An orientation, she explained, was what you had if you didn't like doing *it*. Her dad had told her. So obviously Ms Pringle – who had confessed to becoming pregnant carefully and responsibly because of her orientation – had gone to a sperm bank. Jennifer didn't want to admit that she didn't know what that was. Naturally she knew both what sperm was and what a bank was, but she had some difficulty with the apposition. It was not that her conception of a bank was a childish one. A bank, she understood, was not just a place that helped you save up for a rainy day. Somehow, it could also lend your money to someone else while you still had it in the bank. Clearly something like that would be necessary with sperm too. But then there was the problem of how a man actually put his sperm in the bank. According to *Life: The Facts, Book One: Responsible Loving*, sperm comes out when a man does *it* with a woman, but preferably not too soon. It then gets caught in his condom, which he wears to communicate to her that he values and respects her. So he must have to take his condom to the bank afterwards, where it gets hung up or poured out into a jar. But *why* did he want to save it in the first place? Most men didn't, judging from the local park.

On the surface, this is the kind of question a child might ask any responsible adult. Hence Jennifer might have asked her mother. In fact, part of her wanted to – the part that could reasonably be called her curiosity. But a different part of her which didn't have a name like that, or not one she knew of, wanted to ask her father instead.

Mary had not yet told Jennifer about the scheduled meeting. Wisely, she would do so only after the event, and then only if everything turned out for the best. There was no point in putting Jennifer on tenterhooks for the next twenty hours, let alone raising the child's hopes only for them to be cruelly dashed.

It was not that she had thought this through in any strictly cogitative sense. Maternal correctness had become instinctive for Mary.

At twenty-one, fresh from university with a degree in Communication Studies, she had felt the world was her oyster – so much so that it had taken eighteen months for her transferable skills to find their niche in it. Marriage followed in due course. When Jennifer came along, she had had no regrets in choosing full-time motherhood. In post-feminist Britain this was like becoming an honorary member of a new aristocracy, apart from being the right thing to do. Above all she looked forward to being at the school gates a good ten minutes early and sharing with other full-timers their compassion for the emotionally impoverished children of career girls. Then there would be babysitting circles which offered far more than the mere chance to get out once a fortnight, such as regular coffee mornings to revise membership criteria. And the environment would benefit from the natural choice of re-usable nappies – provided you used a green detergent, of course.

She had never regretted opting out of the rat race. No one is indispensable in the cut and thrust of the war of attrition called commerce, at least at high street branch level, but you can't say the same about parenting. True, there had been times when she felt more like chief cook and bottle washer. But nothing is perfect, is it?

What she did think through concerned her own hopes. One of these saw John's deepest motive (whether he knew it or not) as being to recapture conjugal bliss, rather than to re-establish responsible fatherhood. In that sense the main item on the agenda was of less direct concern to Jennifer, although she would, of course, be a beneficiary.

But this line of thought was a potential quicksand, so Mary stepped back from its brink. '*If* marital or even just domestic bliss is what he now wants,' she told herself, 'I still mustn't forgive him before he even gets here. No, at the very least I've got to grind a number of axes and read the riot act. But I never was very good at playing hard to get.'

The bottles in which sparkling wines are kept are distinct both in shape and seal from those that house even the most up-market vins de table. No doubt down to earth, solidly practical reasons lie behind this. But form and function sometimes coincide not only in a pleasing aesthetic but also in symbolic significance. The shape which best contains a wine under pressure is, at the shoulders, more Barbara Hepworth than Henry Moore, so much so that no clear line can be drawn between the body and the neck. The eye is therefore drawn upwards rather than downwards, to a point (the cork) which speaks of fun as against work (no corkscrew being needed). The overall effect is spiritually uplifting and suggests that youth can, after all, be recaptured.

John had initially thought of saying it with flowers, but he arrived with a bottle of Asti Spumante instead. The logic was that this could be drunk. He did not expect this to happen immediately, of course (indeed, given the problem of in vino veritas, it would be prudent to wait), not necessarily even later that same day. Even so, to Mary the gesture appeared to be jumping the gun. Pointedly, she put it on top of, rather than in, the fridge.

"Like the hair-do. It's you to a T," John countered.

"Make yourself at home, John."

Contrary to plan, this didn't generate enough tension to notice, let alone to cut with a knife. By taking off his shoes and sitting on the sheepskin rug by the radiator, John did as she commanded as if he would have done so anyway.

149

After an exchange of formalities – "How has life been treating you?"... "I can't complain. And you?"... "Oh, keeping myself busy and thereby any torrid time at bay" – which both knew were but the calm before the storm, silence reigned. John felt its regal finger pointing in his direction. Soon, it became abundantly clear that Mary was not even going to say "Well?" He was on his existential own as far as broaching the subject was concerned. What could he do but boldly go where none had been before him (at least with this rejected female of the species)?

It was as Mary had foreseen. John had come round to the idea of spending more time with his family. But he also wanted Mary to accept him for what he was. In one sense this meant that he had nothing to apologise for, while in another sense, of course, he was ready and willing to do so. It also meant that he sought closure on a matter that needed setting the record straight. He had considered various roundabout ways of doing so, but since in the final analysis all came down to being upfront, and since there's no time like the present for not putting things off any longer, he had decided to throw caution to the wind and to admit to having been economical with the truth, even to having resorted, albeit fleetingly, to alternative facts, thus leaving Mary in the dark concerning certain circumstances at the time of his departure – although these were not now, nor had they ever been, of the essence.

John felt acutely aware that he was batting on a sticky wicket. But that was better than skating on thin ice. Honesty really is the best policy – but you still have to play your cards right.

"So there *was* someone else?"

"Yes."

The confession made, routine questioning followed.

"How old?"

"It's immaterial."

"The truth will out."

"It's not the heart of the matter."

"It's part of the shit that must hit the fan."

"It's not the core issue."

But for Mary, no holds were barred.

"The can of worms is *open*, John. *How old?*"

"Twenty-something... I think."

"Men are pathetic!"

John did his best to look bloody but unbowed.

"There are two sides to every story."

"Not to the unvarnished truth."

"I needed to embrace a new life experience."

"You mean you needed to embrace a new..."

"It's not so simple."

"You're only as old as the woman you feel. It's that simple."

"I've never thought of you as past your sell-by date."

"But familiarity breeds contempt."

"I felt stuck in a rut."

"So you went to plough another furrow."

"All right. But not to sow any wild oats."

"Just to make hay while the sun shines."

"Fun and games were strictly incidental."

"Don't ask me to think the unthinkable."

"What's that?"

"That you were head over heels in love."

"Of course not. I may have had my head in the clouds now and then, but I kept my feet on the ground."

"Was she... good looking?"

"Up to a point. Not the crème de la crème, but I wasn't scraping the barrel."

"More attractive than me?"

"Comparisons are odious."

"So I didn't even cross your mind, when..."

"I mean I'm not the kind of man who thinks in terms of good or bad legs, let alone how nearly they approach the armpits, or good or mediocre breasts, let alone their quantity to the pound. I see the whole person. A person is a person is a package. Everyone is unique."

Mary's cat and mouse game had paid off. John had just walked into what might, at a pinch, have been a trap.

"Maybe. And maybe beauty is in the eye of the beholder. But that doesn't apply to the *age factor*, does it? Why, John, why?"

"Why what, exactly?"

"Why with a *mere girl*? Have you *no pride*?"

"Any excuse in what, I admit, is a common or garden situation is bound to seem tired, limp or lame. So I'm not making any. But I'd like to make it clear that she was *not* young enough to be my daughter, except in a biological sense, nor did I once lose sight of what research shows, that women reach their sexual peak in their thirties."

"Well, I'm not going to demean myself by asking for a blow by blow account of *her* performance (that's the word men use, I believe). It's beneath my dignity to inquire into the number, degree or even the means of expression of her orgasms."

John passed on this one.

"All I want to know is, what did she have – dubious charms, dulcet tones, dark desires – that I don't have? A lost, innocent look, perhaps?"

"Mary, you're barking up the wrong tree."

"Oh? And I suppose I've got the wrong end of the stick too?"

"Yes. It's not a question of *you* and what you have or haven't got. It's not a question of *her* and what she has or hasn't got (I mean had or hadn't got). It's a question of *me*. There was something in *me*, trying to get out! Mary, listen to me! Try to understand! I seemed so near and yet so far from being... *me*. None of this was to boost my *ego*. It was to find *myself*. I saw myself as turning into the man on the Clapham omnibus, slowly but surely, Joe Soap incarnate, worse, A. N. Other himself.... I just had to jump in at the deep end – God, this is so difficult to put into words – the deep end of *myself*. To find out if *my* still waters ran deep. Or if I was just an empty swimming pool of a man."

John was beginning to make the running. He might even have found her Achilles' heel. In Mary's armoury, anyway, derision was not a strong point. Worse, she wanted to believe him. That's natural enough, of course, but why show it?

"But why couldn't you plumb your hidden depths in the comfort of your own home – with me?"

"Do you think I'd have been able to take the plunge of *writing a novel* if I'd never moved out? Do you think I'd have been able to move out *just* to be able to take that plunge? I would never have been able to hurt you like that."

"Oh, I see. And moving out because of a *younger woman*, I mean a *mere girl*, would be less in the way of a devastating blow?"

"Mary, you're forgetting something. I didn't tell you about her."

"How considerate. You know what hurts me most, John? What really, really hurts? That you didn't feel able to *share* something with me. I *like* novels!"

"I can explain."

"Can you?"

"Yes. I had a novel inside me, true enough. But I was unaware of the fact. Oblivious would be the wrong word. On the unconscious level, I must have had an inkling. It was, so to speak, that inkling that I was unaware of. Hence I wasn't able to share it."

John had climbed out of the frying pan, only to find himself back in the fire.

"In other words, you moved out because of *her*."

"I moved out to find out why I had to move out. A thought experiment wouldn't have worked, in the circumstances."

She had reduced him to ducking and diving. It was time to get him up against the ropes.

"Face up to it, John. Say it like it is. Don't think you can finesse it. I can tell the spin from the spun. Call a spade a spade for once in your life. Don't imagine you can pull the wool over my eyes. I wasn't born yesterday. What you had to find out was whether you preferred *her* or *me*. That's it, isn't it? And now she's solved that knotty little problem for you, hasn't she? By walking out on you. By dumping you."

"That's a gross oversimplification."

Mary was on a roll. "Actions speak louder than words, John. The habit doesn't make the monk, you know. Nor can the leopard change its spots. You are what you are. You didn't even show moderation in excess! Tell me, twenty-*what*?"

"Mary, you're working on the assumption that fidelity is love in action. It would be, in a perfect world. But into every life a little rain must fall. You know why? That's how we *grow!* Life isn't easy. Sometimes we're on our own, blind to our own true selves – without even the blind to lead us!"

"And now it's back to the bargain basement, to the little woman put on the back burner, left on the shelf, definitely non-scene, a domestic convenience, better than a slap in the face with a wet fish, she'll come round, after a little wailing and gnashing of teeth, she'll just count to ten, she'll swallow anything, hook, line and sinker, a born masochist, the victim type, desperate for affection, lost, confused..."

"Mary, you have every right to be upset."

"Let me finish!"

"All right."

"Thank you. ... low in self-esteem, unable to enjoy her own company, unable to say No, unable to mean No when she says it, unconditional, unquestioning love her only asset. *That's* it, isn't it?"

"No."

"Hand on heart?"

"Yes."

"Good. Because that's not me... any longer."

A sudden, reckless impulse seized Mary. She would tell him about Ron! Little did she care that that would be a Pyrrhic victory if ever there was one. Little did she care that she would thereby win the battle but lose the war. Fortunately, John saved her from herself. It was time for his keynote speech.

"What *I* ask, Mary," he went on, having just (as he saw it) given her something she wanted, "is that you try to look beneath the surface of what, in the eyes of the world, is a cliché. I'm not just *any* forty-something man who left his wife (temporarily) for the sake of a younger woman. In my case, the younger woman was a means to an end. Not that the end necessarily justifies the means. Nor, I admit, does this way of stating the case necessarily transcend the usual cliché scenario. But my defence (if I can put it like that) rests, firstly, on the fact that no other means occurred to me at the time and, secondly, on the claim that the end was not run of the mill. There just isn't a *right phrase* for it, in fact. It was not, as I said before, to boost my ego, nor to add spice to my life. How can I put it? In a strange way she, the 'younger woman' as you label her, was a means to the end of discovering *why* she was not the end. In that sense I needed to live the experience of discovering where exactly I had gone wrong. But insofar as I had gone wrong, I had done so in the knowledge that, in a roundabout way, it would lead somewhere right and in that paradoxical sense going wrong was at least a way of getting on the right track. Naturally I couldn't explain any of this to you at the time, for the simple reason that I couldn't explain it to myself. My conscience pricked me, of course, but deep inside I kept my self-respect. Getting inside the panties of another party wasn't the be all and end all, more the lesser of two evils. I dislike the Americanism intensely, but if I had not 'cheated on' you, I would have been cheating myself. In that sense, I fully admit, I acted out of self-interest – but the justifiable self-interest of self-discovery. Ask yourself, would you have been happy with the empty shell of a husband, a man who had looked before he leapt and, as a result, had gone on living a lie, pottering aimlessly about the house, putting a brave face on his taedium vitae, increasingly finding marriage a poisoned chalice, taking refuge in the demon drink or other mood moderators, spiritually dead and even incapable of taking any life-enhancing initiative? No, Mary, no, in the context of the bigger picture I've not been irresponsible. I've just not been as solid as a rock, not to mention a safe pair of hands, from *your* point of view. I've made my bed and I'm prepared to lie in it. Just separate the wood from the trees, you'll see: there's no fundamental reason for you not to get into that bed with me."

Mary felt that somewhere along the line she must have missed the chance to come down on him like a ton of bricks. Now there would be no knock-out blow. She needed to devise some kind of face-saving formula instead.

"You're overlooking one giant among trees: hell hath no fury like a woman left in splendid isolation."

John was glad she had varied the expression. Irony was a positive sign. A little submission became the order of the day.

"Naturally I don't expect you to turn a blind eye."

"Just the other cheek."

"No. I realise you've had a raw deal. I realise I've ridden roughshod over your sensitivities. I realise I've put you through the mangle emotionally. I'm prepared to reap the whirlwind."

"Well, that's a step in the right direction."

"A great leap forward, even?"

"You're asking me to forgive and forget, to kiss and make up, to welcome you back with open arms? It's not that easy, John."

"I see. More a case of one step at a time, then?"

"Yes. The past is the past, but it's not yet dim and distant, is it? Yes, tomorrow is another day, but it also never comes. I know, sometimes it's necessary to let bygones be bygones. But you can't wipe the slate clean. You can't run away from yourself. You have to live with your mistakes."

"To err is human, to forgive divine. As I see it, our marriage is definitely *not* a case of it's all over bar the shouting."

In her heart of hearts, Mary knew they were made for each other. To all intents and purposes, John had put his finger on a foregone conclusion. But for the time being she had regained the upper hand. She didn't want to over-egg the pudding, but she wasn't averse to moving the goalposts now and then.

"John, I'm saying this more in sorrow than in anger. Once a man strays..."

"You mean it's a slippery slope?"

"Well, once bitten, twice shy."

"I understand that your faith in me has been seriously challenged. I realise that being left in the lurch has left you wary of what's on the horizon. But there's a sincere team player in me waiting to get out. I'm fully prepared to knuckle down to the nuts and bolts of relationship rebuilding."

"You're not just paying lip service to the idea of caring and sharing?"

"It's not such a paradigm shift, you know. There's no call for habit reversal. I won't be playing a new role on the domestic stage. More of an old one. And by the book."

"That's not good enough."

"Oh?"

"What makes you think I was happy before?"

"Regular statements to that effect. Smiles. That sort of thing."

"That was contentment. Now I want something more."

"Is it within my power, scope or remit?"

"That remains to be seen."

"I hope it's not going to cost an arm and a leg."

"Not financially, no."

Vision and game plans were up for discussion, it seemed. They would now look to the future, not dig up the past. He wouldn't be consigned to history, nor even put on ice. Mary only had to lay it on the line, he'd see what he could do to toe it. Any Yes Man role would be short term. He even felt prepared to jump through the odd hoop.

"Fire away."

"First, the Golf. It stays in my name. You'll be able to use it, of course (if you don't lose your licence, that is) – when I don't need it."

"Your wish is my command."

"Second, the bathroom needs retiling (the cerulean adds depth but it's on the cold side), the floorboards in that corner don't feel at all safe (I suggest we take the long-term view and replace them) and the lighting scheme in here is too either-or."

"I thought you said it wouldn't cost."

"I'm thinking DIY."

"I see. Go on."

"I want you to notice that kind of thing for yourself. I don't want to have to keep telling you what to do. I don't want to feel that I have to nag."

As behavioural contracting goes, this was pushing it. John summoned up a note of irritation – but it's not much consolation to save one's face in one's own eyes only.

"Naturally. Of course not. Anything else?"

"Yes. One thing."

"And what might that be?"

"Your novel."

"My novel?"

"Yes. I want you to... think of a different title."

"Why?"

"Oh, no reason."

"Your whim is my command too, is that it?"

"No. I want you to do it for me."

"Any suggestions?"

"I'd have to read it."

"Why? You find the existing title off-message without having perused any portion."

"It just makes me feel uneasy."

"I see."

"What do you see?"

"If that's how you think of me...."

"I don't follow."

"How about *The Worm That Returned*, or *The Worm That Left the Straight and Narrow... for a While*?"

"John, you don't understand. I don't think of *you* as a worm. Or if I do, it's as the *dangerous* kind."

"Hm."

"I know I'm being silly, but please."

Given her strong hand, "please" had not been de rigueur. It touched him deeply.

"I would if I could, Mary. Believe me, I'd like to do it for you. But there'd be no point. At best, it would be an empty gesture. You see... the novel will never see the light of day – not even in the form of rejection slips."

"But why?"

"It wasn't going anywhere. From a commercial point of view, the plot was a dead-end. The only course of action open to my large as life but twice as natural hero would have failed to engage the sympathy of Josephine Public (women making up the bulk of avid readers). No, it's a case of return to square one – some day. Of course, nothing is wasted. I've gained useful experience. I've honed up the old craft a bit. As they say, a writer's most important tool is his wastepaper bin. Mine runneth over."

"What a pity."

"Oh, I don't know. I've got home improvements to keep me out of mischief. Laying new foundations in the shape of new floorboards puts me squarely on the side of the angels, I'd say."

"But then... in what sense did you discover your true self, precisely? Which required walking out on me, that is?"

"How can I put it? Yes. Giving free rein to flights of fancy, via the mirror of the blank page, was, in the last analysis, a know-thyself-thing, paving the way to me becoming the author of my own destiny."

Did John feel embarrassed at this formulation? Who knows? At any rate, he felt the time ripe to move onto the next item on the agenda. "But let's not talk about that now. Words, words, words – in the words of Hamlet. There are *other things* in life."

"No, John. Not yet."

"Another time then. We'll make tomorrow the first day of the rest of our lives, shall we?"

"Perhaps. Tell me. Why *did* you choose that title?"

"It chose me, I believe."

"Something suggested it to you, didn't it?"

"Sounds a reasonable hypothesis."

"But it wasn't just the *common expression.*"

"That suggested it to me, you mean? By suggesting *itself*, so to speak?"

"It was that pub."

"Pub?"

"More specifically, the inn-sign."

"Inn-sign?"

"And the story behind it."

"Story behind it?"

"You *must* remember. The story Ron told us."

"Ron?"

"Yes. But perhaps you don't remember, after all. You could have blanked it out, I suppose, in response to the shock."

"Ron?"

"The AA man, you know. First he told us his name – I'm fairly sure it was Ron – then he told us that story. When we had the accident."

"Let's see if I remember it when you tell me. You've got me worried."

"Oh, it's not important."

"I just hope it *is* shock."

"What else?"

"Old age."

John hadn't just returned to the fold! He'd returned to his old self! The appealing or sympathetic-ear-oriented note in the way he had said "old-age" was distinctly pre-crisis. Mary felt something tugging her heartstrings. It was love, which knows that it is more blessed to reassure than to be reassured.

"John, the best is yet to come, you know. As long as you're young at heart – and in good health, of course – life is for living. You haven't got one foot in the grave. It's not *even* time to say there's life in the old dog yet. You're not over the hill. There's nothing decrepit, not even 'wrinkly,' in being mature enough to plan your pension. We're not yet participants in the greying of society. The demographic time-bomb, maybe. But there's no use crying over *future* spillages of milk, is there? Of course, I'm not advocating any live now pay later attitude. Enjoying life means striking a proper balance between living in the present and things that usually involve making lists.... But basically... what I'm trying to say is... I find you very attractive and I don't mind if I do."

And so they did.

For Mary, it was just like old times. How easy it is to forgive, she thought, even without wholesale forgetting. A bitter taste would rise in her gorge on odd occasions, needless to say, but it wouldn't be left in her mouth. It would be nice (there was no other word for it) to have a man around the house again, as against one who simply came around as and when fancy tickled. And when John had gone on to say, "I hope there's more where *that* came from," it had had the ring of truth. Yes, when all was said and done, full-scale reunion was best for both of them.

Not to mention Jennifer.

TWENTY-ONE

It was back to normalcy (at least, it would be as of tomorrow when John moved back in), so the most normal thing to do was to watch the news on TV.

Top of the bill was the fact that the cost of buildings insurance was set to rise substantially for everyone. This was due to various factors including the spiralling cost of buildings. A spokesperson for Aviva explained that insurance was basically like saving up for a rainy day, but that in recent years it had never rained but it poured. It was no longer feasible to increase the premiums only of those at direct risk of flooding, since this might result in economic migrant status for much of the lowland population.

'Oh, dear,' thought Mary. 'Peace of mind is such a basic necessity. I'm afraid that puts a place in the sun out of the question.'

Jennifer came back from her grandmother's just in time for the item deemed second in newsworthiness. The recent winner of the popular 'existential show,' *Hell is Other People*, had been charged with driving without due care and attention. Viewers were then treated to two minutes of highlights of Nathan Smiley's meteoric rise to stardom. Jennifer thought he looked quite like her new, young, male teacher, Mr Winsom. She wondered whether hoping against hope that Ms Pringle might discover the joys of full-time motherhood meant that she (Jennifer, not Ms Pringle) was experiencing first love. But it could just be infatuation.

"Jennifer, I've got some news for you," said her mother.

"Shhhh!"

"All right. Be like that."

Television, of course, is an important unifying factor in the global village. Hence others were watching too, at the very same time.

Angela, however, was only half-watching, for she was also preparing a new paper. The Darwinian or Dawkinsian imperative in academic life was uppermost in her mind. Publish or perish. Pass on your memes in print or end up merely teaching undergrads. The topic was not as yet fully defined, but the title – "Transgendering the Sphinx: Textual *His*-tericism in 'later' Virginia Woolf" – was. But her train of thought was distracted by the third item of that day's news.

"The debate over global warming seems to be 'hotting up'," said the newsreader, with a knowing smile. "The Minister for Public Opinion had to stand in today at a conference in Oxford for the Minister for the Environment – who had been urgently called to open a state of the art retail therapy centre just outside the village of Walmondsley, just outside Grantham, which was finished two full weeks ahead of the expiry of a six-month delay. One climo-boffin became especially 'hot under the collar' when the Minister suggested that current doomsday scenarios were creating panic, especially among old people. They had a right to live out their twilight years, he informed delegates, without always being constantly reminded of the fact that time was fast running out for any genes they had successfully passed on. The scientist, a seventy-five year-old specialist on West Antarctic ice sheet bacteria with five grandchildren and two great grandchildren then stood up and called out, 'My father lived to a hundred and four! If I live that long I'll have great-great-great grandchildren – but they'll only have a life-expectancy of twelve and a half!' It took two plain clothes private security guards and a chaos theorist to drag him from the hall."

Angela's attention was initially caught by the reference to Oxford, but quickly embraced the specific topic. Climate change, she reflected, was a discourse predicated on the seventeenth century *faith* that there was just one 'real world' 'out there' which was 'knowable'. To her, however, 'climate change' was a narratorial-superstructure on the imaginary meta-phenomenal level *underpinned* ideologically by an anxiety crisis in the patriarchal myth of man's domination over 'nature' – at least, that was what it was until something actually *went wrong*.

Any lingering memory of John didn't get a look in.

Mary senior saw the same story differently. 'Twilight years,' she ruminated. 'Twilight years! Who *does* he think he is? That last increase in the pension was insulting. No one in the government even remembers the war, that's the trouble. The sacrifices we made. The shortages we went through. The rationing. Long hot summers. Spitfires in a clear blue sky. Yes, the weather was definitely better then. But I expect it always is when you're a child.' (Truth to tell, she had been born as late as 1945, but a full two months *before* VE Day so she had a natural tendency to extend 'the war' until approximately 1953.)

Ranked four was the second reading of the 'Membership of Trades Unions, Private Militias and Religious Cults' Bill, which would make it compulsory for anyone wishing to join a trade union first to sit an hour-long examination consisting of fifty multiple-choice questions about British history and British values. Speaking in the Commons the Prime Minister said that "as a true One Nation Tory and, I might add, *ex-scholarship* girl who has actually experienced the psychological stresses and social humiliations of *just about managing*, albeit as an undergraduate, I totally reject the risible conspiracy theory promulgated by the Leader of the Opposition that this legislation is aimed at further slashing real wages and bulldozing vestigial workers' rights. Let me remind the Right Honourable gentleman," she went on, "that what he calls 'a race to the bottom' and what the IMF refers to purely academically as 'labour market reform' is in fact good old-fashioned competition! And since this former workshop of the world no longer thinks quality, and any after-sales service worthy of the name has become a logical paradox, then *price-competitiveness* is the only game in town!"

Ron was not convinced. In his younger days he had actively endorsed, more or less, the maxim that although philosophers had been content to interpret the world, the point was to change it. But after chancing upon and dipping into Francis Fukuyama's *The End of History and the Last Man*, he'd come to feel that the question 'What is to be done?' had become rhetorical, a shrug. It seemed to have been replaced, as a question in search of an answer, by 'Where did we go wrong?' In any case, he was a loner at heart; unity is strength was a self-evident truth, but one that left him out of its loop. He was a rolling stone, not quite footloose and fancy free, but content with his own company. Hence he had taken to the road, a walking (or rather driving) paradigm of de-industrialization. In consequence the once-in-a-lifetime near meltdown of capitalism in 2008 had largely passed him by, for he had been in process of discovering a new side of himself by engaging on a day-to-day basis with mere breakdowns instead. He had once said so to Mary.

"The need to offer a helping hand to those who're in distress," he had explained. "As I see it, this job connects me to the underlying British tradition. I don't say English, note. I'm talking Celtic rather than Anglo-Saxon. I'm not one to blow my own trumpet, but I like to feel that something in the Arthurian legends lives on through me."

But not faith. Not truth, in that awkward other sense of the word. He couldn't sit still, emotionally. His best practice was errant. Let others call that erring. For him, there was no U-turn in life for the simple reason that there was no U-look. Not so much as a glance over the shoulder.

Which brings us to John. But not for long, because he was not watching. He was in his bedsit packing up, where neither a TV nor the bandwidth to watch online were among the bare necessities. He did have an old radio, but news on the radio is not like a play or a football match. It does not engage the listener's imaginative faculty. On the contrary, the medium of radio tends to reduce the news to mere information, contextualisation and analysis.

Elsewhere, the small screen continued to dissect matters of public concern.

Shane Randall and Susy Cute had announced that they had agreed on a divorce, after weeks of intense media speculation. The fifty-four year-old breakfast TV host had confessed to having wanted numerous affairs during the year-long marriage, while the lead singer for Popcorn said she had just not been ready at seventeen for medium term commitment. When asked if the age gap had been too much, Shane acknowledged that he had sometimes misinterpreted Susy's need to be cuddled while Susy admitted that sometimes she had reacted over-ironically to Shane's sciatica.

Even Louise failed to understand why these two had hitched up in the first place. Such coverage of a storm in a teacup, as marital dissolutions went, downgraded the very idea of divorce. It might even become part of the current zeitgeist that divorce was a piece of cake, something you could get through DIY, with only a Readers' Digest Quintessential Guide.

"Any news of John these days? On the magnum opus in progress, for example?"

Howard had been asking too many questions about John lately, even apropos of nothing in particular. It made Louise feel uneasy. Still, it would help avoid any misunderstandings when John returned to hearth and home. When Louise had "unreservedly anticipated" this of him, John had quickly seen the various pros, with hardly a con entering the frame. His very first words had been, "Howard, I assume, is often out?" She put this down to great minds thinking alike rather than telepathy.

"As far as I know – from Mary, that is – he's an unmitigated bore on the subject."

"They're on talking terms, then?"

"Oh, yes. Picking up on some subtle cues, I have a distinct feeling that very soon he'll no longer be persona non grata back in the homestead. You just mark my words."

"'Unmitigated bore' being your take, presumably, then?" Howard deduced.

"To state the obvious."

Next, a new quasi-governmental body had been set up charged to investigate abuses of self-regulation. It had no powers of enforcement, but it would be able to request that its recommendations be given all due consideration. Self-regulation was a central plank of government policy. In time, concepts such as freedom of speech and freedom of association were to be replaced by self-regulation of speech and self-regulation of association. This would not apply to political demonstrations, which would continue to be humanely policed. The government's strategy was to instil a sense of corporate responsibility not only in corporations but in British culture as a whole.

But have we run out of characters?

No, for fortunately there is still Ms Pringle (although she made only a brief personal appearance long ago in Part One, and that purely in her professional capacity), who had recently brought a new life into the world.

Ms Pringle had the volume low because Ollie was her very first child and she did not yet realise that a sleeping baby is deaf to the world. She wondered (not for the first time) whether self-regulation was acceptable or unacceptable – as a phrase. Certainly it was easier to understand the concept of abuse of self-regulation than it was that of abuse of freedom. On the other hand an abuse of self-regulation was not actually an abuse *of* self-regulation, but an abuse of one or more living human beings. It was always necessary to remind oneself of that fact, when using the word 'abuse'. In that sense the phrase sugared the pill, rather like 'Pax Americana,' 'conviction politician' or 'boys will be boys'.

She now had an enhanced sense of the phrase 'living human being,' so she looked at Oliver without yet thinking of him explicitly as a 'boy'. He seemed so autonomous. Of course, she recognised his dependence on her. He was not autonomous in the sense of being fully self-regulating. But he was complete. He had five fingers on each of two hands, five....

All-importantly, he had a future. He would grow up to become the central character in his very own story. Just like John.

But for now another episode in the daily soap, with its multiple plots, exotic settings and larger than life characters, was drawing to its conclusion, not with a cliff hanger but some kind of positive reinforcement. For this was not Fiction. It was Life – if not exactly as we know it. It aroused pity and fear, but catharsis does not come naturally in the domain of the real. Think, for example, of Oedipus as a real individual who really did kill his father and really did marry his mother and, worse, really did find out these gory details. Then think of this as a story on the news. Great shock-horror. But nothing more sublime.

Hence all had ended well for Leonora, the circus lioness who had become a celebrity because of a bad case of tooth decay. The cavities were large and only mercury fillings would hold. Unfortunately, these would undermine the image of savage ferocity so essential to her show business career, as of course would extraction. But at the eleventh hour Leonora had been spared the lethal injection by Petifare, the pet food company, who said they could use her in a campaign to launch their new 'purr-ee' range.

www.ingramcontent.com/pod-product-compliance
Lightning Source LLC
Chambersburg PA
CBHW030256130626
46549CB00002B/560